TEETH

Fred Stenson

COTEAU BOOKS

Edited by Dave Margoshes.
Cover painting, watercolour pencil crayon on board, by Rob MacDougall, 1994.
Cover design by Dik Campbell.
Book design and typesetting by Val Jakubowski.
Printed and bound in Canada.

Some of the stories in this collection have appeared previously in periodicals and anthologies: "Teeth" appeared first in *Edmonton Magazine*, January, 1982; "Positive Images" appeared in the anthology *Alberta Rebound* (NeWest Press, 1990); "Place of Pain" appeared in *Dandelion*, 1992; "Burns Burns Burns and Burns" appeared in *Canadian Fiction Magazine*, 1992; "Hitting the Monkey" appeared in *Quarry Magazine*, 1993.

The publisher gratefully acknowledges the financial assistance of the Saskatchewan Arts Board, the Canada Council, the Department of Canadian Heritage, and the City of Regina Arts Commission.

Canadian Cataloguing in Publication Data

Stenson, Fred, 1951-

Teeth

ISBN 1-55050-060-0

I. Title.

PS8586.T45T4 1994   C813'.54   C94-920170-7
PR9199.3.S74T4

COTEAU BOOKS
401-2206 Dewdney Ave.
Regina, SK   S4R 1H3

*For Sheila
and for my children,
Ted and Kate*

DOUG BURNS

265

C · BISONS

HEIGHT: 6'0"   WEIGHT: 178   SHOOTS: RIGHT
Acquired: 1st Round Choice 1984 Draft
Born: 12-22-65, Beaver Creek, AB

NHL RECORD · FICHE DANS LA LNH

YEAR ANNÉE	TEAM ÉQUIPE	GP	G	A	PTS	PIM
84-85	Bisons	80	12	10	22	2
85-86	Bisons	80	26	21	47	0
86-87	Bisons	80	35	23	58	4
87-88	Bisons	80	23	16	39	14
NHL TOTALS/ TOTAUX DANS LA LNH		320	96	70	166	20

GAME WINNING GOALS/ BUTS GAGNANTS 1984-88: 1

Bison's first choice in 1984 draft
Premier choix des Bisons lors du repêchage 1984

PLAYOFF RECORD · FICHE DURANT LES ÉLIMMINATOIRES

	GP	G	A	PTS	PIM
Career Carriére		(no playoff experience) (aucune expérience des séries éliminatoires)			

Contents

Teeth

SIXTEEN MINUTES AND SEVEN SECONDS ARE GONE IN the third period of this hockey game. We are behind four to three. The score might suggest to some that we have had a titanic struggle here but we have not. Of the seven goals scored, five went in accidentally off skates and legs. Our goalie slipped and fell on one of the other two.

If the technicians who are steadily creeping into this game ever equip players with a device for clocking average speed (an innovation I suspect and dread), this would show up as a far slower than average game. It's a Tuesday night not long after Christmas, and all around me I see that fatigued, glassy look that tells me that the rest of the players, like myself, are lapsing into a low energy coma. At the end of the game, they might have to move all this meat off the bench with a stock prod.

They say that some people play this game for fun. I personally can't imagine it and suspect it of being something cooked up by the owners and the press. I do have a foggy recollection of thirteen-year-old kids flailing away on corner lots in the freezing cold for reasons other than money or coercion, but I also know that I was never one of them.

My parents gave me no choice in the matter. They drove me to the rink late at night or at dawn, and counted themselves the finest parents in the land for doing so. The fact that I didn't like hockey was unimportant. I was taught to believe that it was something you did whether you liked it or not – like school and community cleanup. For some parents, it's religion or music lessons but my parents wanted neither Christian nor concert musician. They wanted a big, mean pro hockey player who would wish them toothless Happy Birthdays during the Hockey Night in Canada intermissions of their autumn years.

"Burns! Go on! C'mon, get the hell out there!"

Amazing. For a moment, I totally forgot where I was. All the hockey rinks and benches of my life merged into one and I didn't know whether I was twelve, eighteen or twenty-five – a bantam, a junior or in the NHL.

The truth is that I'm in the NHL and that I'm on our toasty warm home bench. The man yelling at me is Chip, our coach and general manager, all crimson with rage. He is yelling because my line didn't go on when the other line came off. For many seconds now, there has been no one on the ice but our goalie and six members of the other team.

One of them shoots. Carrasco, our goalie, gets a leg on it. Another one shoots. He stops that too. We are all cheering now, like mad, but still not one of our players climbs over the boards to play!

"I mean it, Burns! Get in there right now or I'll rip your arms off!"

There is a blood vessel on Chip's forehead, big and beating like an exposed heart. I climb over the boards and my linemates follow. Just in time to see the third rebound come off Carrasco's pad right onto the stick of one of the five players buzzing around his net. The stick flicks, Carrasco dives, but the puck pops over him and into the net. The red light goes on just as we arrive.

Fishing the puck out of the net, I look through the eye apertures of Carrasco's mask. He has drawn stitch marks on the plastic each time it saved him from a killing blast to the face. The mask looks like a railway map of southern Britain. From a distance, this motif is ghoulish, but from this close I can see Ronnie's eyes behind. They are red, watery and scared.

"Where were you guys?" he croaks, a dribble of water running out the bottom of the mask onto his padded chest.

I hand him the puck. "Souvenir, Ronnie. You were terrific." I whack him on the pads and skate to centre ice.

Later, after losing the game 5-3, we sit in the dressing room, grunting orchestrally. There is no mood to this music, happy or sad; it's just there. Heavy breathing in a thought vacuum.

Again I slip quietly off to the ice-bound years of my adolescence. I was on the verge of rebelling, of telling my parents to varnish my hockey stick because it was my last. I was thinking of joining a tribe of travelling potters. I was about to do all that when a scout appeared after one of our playoff games. He took me to the best restaurant in town and told me to order as much of whatever I liked. While I ate, he mentioned several multi-digit money figures and I felt a sudden urge to take my hockey a little more seriously.

But, lately, something has gone wrong. I can't concentrate, not even on money. I just drift off. I start seeing the fifteen-year-old girls who hung around our hockey practices. I can see their faces and memory has edited out every zit. The shy way they used to lurk in the shadows when we came out of the locker room with our hockey bags over our shoulders. I can hear them giggling but I can't hear my own coach when he's screaming, "For the sake of sweet Jesus, get out there!"

Chip enters and slams the door. His hair is sticking up valiantly from its sea of grease. His cheeks are flaming and he brings the smell of whisky in to do battle with the robust aroma of sweat. He stomps up and down between us, his every movement ferocious.

"You guys stunk out there tonight!" he shouts at last, relieving the tension somewhat.

Smitty Smith, the cornerman on my line, wrinkles up his often-smashed nose and gives an attempt at a loud sniff which winds up being a thunderous snort. "Still do," he says, laughing and snorting. "Smell," he adds for the slow ones.

Chip whirls, his coattails winding up like a propeller.

"Who said that?"

"I did, coach," says Smitty.

Poor Smitty, or should I say lucky Smitty because, surely,

hockey is keeping him out of an institution for the criminally stupid. He is regular cannon fodder for Chip's postgame rages. Chip walks up to him and levels a finger at his crooked nose.

"I recently told you idiots that the next time we got scored on because of a slow line change, some lard asses were going to find themselves in the minor leagues. Do you remember that, Smith?"

"No."

"Your line, Smith, was scored on tonight when you weren't even on the goddamn ice!"

"But Burnsy...."

"Screw Burnsy! It was your line and I might just decide to put all three of you idiots down for a while. Maybe in some moose pasture in Maine you'll suddenly remember how to play hockey!"

This is a fairly idle threat. Obviously, Chip would love to send most of us to the minor leagues, and would, except for the total lack of better players there to bring up.

"I'm telling you guys this team's on the verge of a shakeup! Nobody's job is secure as long as we keep losing. There's three things wrong with you. No hustle! No brains! No speed! And no guts!"

"That's four." Smitty grins, not a tooth in his giant head. He is marvellously proud of his deduction.

The effect on Chip is fascinating. He begins to sag slowly, like a pin-punctured inflatable couch. Frowning at the floor, he mutters in a vague monotone, something about the plane we have to catch to Montreal in the morning. He finishes by saying, "If we play like this against Montreal ... " but his voice fades out before he can entirely tell us what we're in for. He shuffles to the door, still sagging. Smitty really can't help himself; he has to give the old coach just one more helping hand.

"They'll kill us," he offers cheerfully.

Hearing Smitty, Chip finds one last nerve of fury yet unexploded. He swings around. His eyes travel the benches on which we sit. I wouldn't be surprised if there are tiny cross hairs in the middle of his vision. When his eyes meet mine, they stop. He pushes the button marked Torpedo.

"Burns. In my office after you shower."

4

When I step into Chip's office a half hour later, he is gnawing on one of his hands. A lonely cannibal. If Chip's stomach was a garbage bag, you wouldn't want to carry anything wet or heavy in it.

"You took your sweet time."

I move a dog-eared scouting file off a chair and sit. Chip waits deliberately, hoping the suspense will fill me with shame and regret.

"You're not putting out, Burns."

"I'm the team's highest scorer."

"Look, Burnsy." The use of *Burnsy*, the friendly form of my name, means an appeal to my sporting side. Chip is still under the impression that I have one. "You could do a hell of a lot more for this team. You're a great little hockey player when you want to be. You were a first-round draft pick."

Fire the scout, I think, but I keep this to myself.

"But, cripes, just sitting there during a line change."

"I think it was my inner ear acting up again."

"Okay, all right. Water under the bridge." Such is Chip's obsession with this game, I bet the water under the bridge is frozen and kids with great potential are playing shinny on it.

He looks up, past my head, at a yellowing photograph of his last winning team: juniors he coached to a national final.

"You could lead this team out of the doldrums." His voice takes on a misty monotone. "We wouldn't have to be in the cellar if you'd play your best game. Take charge. Like Bobby Clarke used to. The players look up to you." He pauses, frowns, takes a bite out of his hand. "They look up to you and you infect the whole bunch of them with a lack of desire!"

I feel this is a bit strong. I try to instill in them a sensible lack of hope.

"Don't you ever want to be on the all-star team, Burns?"

The answer to this question is no but I won't break Chip's heart by telling him. The all-star game is sixty minutes of hockey I currently have the luxury of taking or leaving.

"The point is this, Burns, if you don't start putting out, I'm going to have to trade you."

I shrug.

Chip looks heavenward and grasps at the air. Maybe God is lowering him a ladder.

"This rotten damn game! I can remember juniors I coached, big kids, tough as nails, crying their eyes out because they didn't get drafted. And you? Big fat contract. Endorsements. And you couldn't care less if we trade you."

Chip rips open the bottom drawer of his desk and pulls out a whisky bottle. He spins off the top and it bounds across the carpet. He drains off a couple of inches, then drags the back of his hand across his mouth. His eyes are those of a cornered pig.

"What about me? What the hell do I do when I get fired off this tail-end team?"

Perhaps Chip could sell endorsements for ulcer milk:

It was the third period of the game. We were behind and stinking the place out. It would be our sixth loss in a row and I could already hear the management baying for my blood. I can tell you, my ulcers were giving me hell. I reached for the mickey of rye in the inside pocket of my sports jacket but my wife had taken it out and replaced it with a bottle of Abdomal, the Ulcer Milk. My first thought was, that bitch! But when the Abdomal got down there and started to soothe....

"Get out of my sight, Burns! You make me sick."

A speedy jaunt in my Porsche and I am home to my luxurious two-bedroom condo by the river. The kitchen faucet exudes a thin stream of boiling-hot water which in former times was a simple drip. The dirty socks, the Kentucky Fried Chicken bones, the cones of cigar ash on the carpet, the beer bottles lying on their sides....

I had a cleaning lady once. She clucked her tongue and said how disgusting. A monkey wouldn't live like this and you a big-shot hockey player too. As a helping hand to a better life, she stole my liquor.

In the midst of this filth, I sit in almost abject misery. If I was someone looking in, I would sneer. How dare you be abjectly miserable with a salary the size of yours, I'd say. And all I could say back would be a lot of whining about too many practices and road trips, about our gruelling schedule. I would also plead my peculiar belief about the women of this world.

According to the popular myth, there are a million women in this land who are dying to take care of and slip between the satin sheets with me, a national sports hero. I believe in this ghostly battalion of beauties with a kind of desperate fervour. I do my best to keep myself attractive for them. For instance, all thirty-two of my teeth are still straight and solid in their gums – a rarity if not a total exception among hockey players.

My secret is regular brushing, flossing and total avoidance of anything resembling a fight, an elbow or a high stick. It was once said of me by a smart-ass reporter that I could go into the corners with fresh eggs in my hockey pants and never break a one. It's true.

But where are these women? This is the greatest mystery of my life. Maybe they are in bed with my toothless teammates but I doubt it. I have a feeling that they are already married to lawyers and carpenters and accountants, and that they limit their goings-on with pro athletes to a sly lusting after our brutishness in front of the colour TV Saturday night.

But really, as I sit here in my bathrobe, sipping an orange juice past my perfect, mint-flavoured teeth – my jock strap drying on a chair between me and the national news – I look at my purple shins, the scars on my knees and ask, who in their right mind *would* be interested in this body?

Less than twenty hours later, the gate swings open and the Montreal Forum ice gleams ahead of me under the TV lights. Yes, for the first time all season, we are going to be displaying our talents on national TV. At last, our moms and dads across the land will have the opportunity of watching their favourite sons being thrashed by one of the nation's most powerful hockey machines.

We emerge to a chorus of jeers and boos from the rabid Forum fans. Our team name is the Bisons. That always seemed like a prophetic and fitting title for our team. I devised my own little cheer from it to motivate me across dull spots in the play.

> Go Bisons go!
> Big, stupid and slow;
> Onward to'rd extinction,
> Go Bisons go!

The game begins and before it is a minute old, the Canadiens's star right-winger has picked the puck from Steve Burke's skates, gone in alone on Carrasco and popped the puck past his internationally-famous weak spot: low to the stick side.

Soon after, we take a penalty and the Canadiens have us all hemmed in on our own end again. It looks like just a matter of time until they bang in another one. I'm staying out of trouble by the blue line. It's safe and quiet there and a nice short skate to centre ice after the goal.

All of a sudden, one of our defencemen takes a wild swipe at the puck, connects and knocks it rolling up the ice. The Montreal defencemen have all closed in on our net for the kill and, as a result, I am the closest person to the puck by about twenty metres. I skate for it and have perhaps the cleanest breakaway of my professional career.

I try hard to concentrate. I haven't scored a goal in six games and Chip may be getting serious about trading me. A new team might mean pressure, extra practices or, God forbid, the playoffs.

The goalie is coming out to challenge. I should really deke and go around but I might screw up and lose the puck. Better to shoot now. I pick a spot in the right corner and fire. Somehow, I fan. I get practically no wood on the shot at all. But the goalie, seeing what I intended to do, has moved to cover the right-hand corner. This opens up a space between his legs and, through that space, my meagre shot trickles. It has just enough momentum to get over the goal line into the net. The period ends 1-1.

During the intermission, Chip tries to tell us that the Canadiens aren't that tough. We'll take 'em, boys, he says. This is such a good one that several of us cannot stifle laughter.

Halfway through the second period, pucks start streaming past Carrasco's stick side. Every time we make a big effort to stop this shelling, we take a penalty and they pot another one. After the fourth one, Carrasco comes skating over to the bench like a man possessed. He tries to open the door into the bench but Chip is holding it shut from the other side.

"What's wrong with you? You're not hurt."

"Lem'me in," Carrasco whimpers. "I saw it again."

He jerks his mask off. His face is white. A drop of sweat jiggles crazily on the point of his chin. "I saw the ghost again. He had on a white uniform. He skated in on me laughing. His teeth were all black. He slapped the puck and it went right through me! Right in one side and out the other!"

"You stop talking like a nut and get the hell back out there!"

Burke, our captain, leans over. "Gosh, coach, let him come out. He won't stop nothing like this. It's a mental problem."

"You're damn right he's got a mental problem. He can't stop a G.D. thing on his stick side!"

Carrasco stops yanking on the door. He throws his goalie stick up into the crowd and climbs over the boards. He beats his way past Chip and runs on his skates down the alley to the dressing room.

"Fart!" screams Chip. "No one else in this league has half the crazy bastards I do. Bordeaux, get in there."

Bordeaux is our backup goalie, a fuzz-faced kid from Montreal. His hometown is the very last place on earth he ever wanted to appear – on TV yet – playing behind a cheesecloth outfit like the Bisons. But fear drives him to brilliance and the second period ends with no further scoring. 5-1, Canadiens.

In the third period, I score again. If the TV colourman was to discuss my goal after the game, he might describe it this way:

Burns was parked out in front of the net jostling with a defenceman and keeping up a constant stream of chatter. 'Watch it, you bastard, you almost got me in the eye. Hey, ref, this guy's trying to hack my head off here!' All of a sudden, a defenceman on Burns's team winds up for a slapper from the point. It comes in like a bullet and, well, nobody could jump higher on skates than Burns when he thought he was going to get hit by the puck. So there it was: the puck doing about a hundred and Burns up in the air this high; the puck hits his skate blade, whango! and it's in the net. Heck, I must have seen Burns score five goals that way over the years.

But the colourman won't be discussing my goal as it only serves to make the Habs mad. They come storming back, scoring on poor Bordeaux almost at will. Soon, the Montreal crowd is cheering wildly every time the kid stops a dribbler.

Then it happens. The normally level-headed Steve Burke, our captain who has been on the ice for every Montreal goal, goes nuts. He boards the Canadiens' star winger so hard a pane of plexiglass falls out into the crowd. The star winger drops as if shot and does not move.

The rest is axiomatic. Two Montreal players go for Burke with sticks up and threatening. One of our boys goes in to even up the odds. The referee races over to try and prevent total war. Fat chance. The Montreal star still isn't moving. His eyes are closed. He may be dead. All the Montreal players come storming off the bench, which means that all our players must storm off the bench too.

I am on the bench and would love to stay here. But it just isn't done. All these things are as preordained as the events at a Vatican high mass. I file dutifully onto the ice with my gloves held by the gauntlets and skate around the perimeter of the six fights now in progress, trying to look as unmenacing as possible.

The Montreal star is up now. Unhurt, and forgotten. The crowd that was gasping in fear for his career seconds ago is now too busy watching the fight to notice him skating off. One fight is busy spawning another. Oaths wing hither and thither, in need of bilingual translation. Fans are on their feet, clinging to the glass and crying for blood.

In the midst of all this bloody hubbub, it happens again. I begin to drift. I drift down the thousand or so benches I have sat on and pick up not a sliver. I drift right back to Beaver Creek, the small prairie town where I was allowed to live for a few years before I had to move on to bigger centres and better coaches. I am with a girl I had forgotten existed. Her name is Paulette. We're thirteen and we're in the dark beside the rink. She's letting me put my hand up under her heavy woollen sweater. It is the first time I have ever done this. It is freezing cold out. One of my ears is totally numb. It's so cold Paulette is afraid we might freeze solid. I think one part of me is already afflicted. Paulette is most worried about freezing solid because it would mean that we would be found as we are: with my hand up her sweater.

I am so far gone, so absorbed in these philosophical matters, with Paulette and her sweater, that I hardly notice the kid who races over to me, screeches to a halt in a spray of ice, and grabs hold of my sweater. I hardly see his pimply, writhing face, his madman eyes. I hardly hear the stream of abuse from his toothless mouth. While I am in Paulette's sweater, he is trying to pull mine over my head. Unable to do this and frustrated to total insanity by the faraway seraphic smile on my face, he lowers his head and drives the top of his helmet into my mouth.

This, I feel.

Suddenly Paulette is gone. Her sweater. Beaver Creek. All banished back to the foreign past. The crazy kid is gone too. Dragged off by a referee or by one of my teammates. I am back in the Forum. Standing at centre ice. I look down at the red dot and it is getting redder by the second, dyed by a stream from my mouth. A quick lick tells me that one of my two perfect, well-flossed and brushed front teeth is no longer occupying its traditional place in my healthy gum. I don't remember swallowing it. Slowly, I skate around the ice looking. It's got to be here somewhere. Teeth don't just vanish.

Then I am corralled by our trainer and one of our players. I keep telling them I must find my tooth but they are pushing me along toward the gate.

On the narrow bench in the dressing room. Mouth wadded full

of cotton batting. The muffled roar of the crowd as the game peters out to its lopsided conclusion.

The game ends. The team trudges in. Chip follows, raving about a shakeup. I am not around to be raved at, however. I am off in the near future this time, rather than the distant past I so often visit. In this near future, there are sticks but they are embedded in wienies and the soft bellies of ice cream bars. There are pucks too, of bacon. Body checks come annually at the doctor's office and he always announces that you are in great physical condition. Afterwards, you go home to your pad, an old-fashioned, modest and clean apartment. Meeker is someone more meek than someone else.

Somehow, every time I lick up under my swollen lip, I am reminded of this near future and the many sources from which money can come. Money, unlike teeth, can be replenished. A missing tooth is a hole in your head for life.

Mark My Prophetic Words

P OP GUNN'S CHIN FLOATED COMFORTABLY IN THE broad cushion of his second chin. His eyes, above the cheeks with the red plants growing on them, were closed in the shadow of his fedora brim. When a stewardess, thinking to be helpful, tried to remove the hat, one of Pop's freckled hands leapt up to hold it on. All the same he was asleep and everyone else on the red-eye flight to Montreal was glad.

The jet, plunging east through the night, was carrying hockey's NHL Bisons to the first game of a three-game road trip. They had just completed a five-game Christmas homestand with a record of no wins, four losses and a tie. The headline over Pop Gunn's column in the *Spectator* that morning had read:

NO ONE SAFE IN CURRENT SLIDE

Does any member of this dismal team, any person responsible for its coaching and management, deserve to sleep quietly in his bed tonight?

Whether they deserved to or not, the Bisons gradually began to nod off, one after another, until finally the core of the wakeful was down to four, three players and the head coach.

Easily the most active of these was general manager and head coach Chip Wad. Chip stuck to and peeled himself repeatedly from the normally non-adhesive seat. Coach Wad tended to sweat in the coolest of environments and the evidence gleamed tonight along the furrows and undulations of his prominent forehead. A series of diagrams lay on the seat tray before him and, from time to time, after a furtive check of cabin personnel, he exposed a straw from behind the wide lapel of his plaid jacket and gave it a cheek-caving tug. The straw extended down into the narrow belly of a silver pocket flask. The diagrams, a series of plays to be used against the Montreal Canadiens tomorrow night, produced goal after goal. The two together, flask and diagrams, restored to Coach Wad the one thing no NHL coach can do without: the conviction that his team can and will win.

Behind Coach Wad sat the wakeful team captain, Steve Burke, a cow-eyed giant staring fixedly at his coffee cup. Burke was thinking a swirl of caffeinated and nonsensical thoughts that had in common his captaincy, the team's current losing streak, and discipline – the need for more discipline on the Bisons team. Burke's father had brought him up on the principle that hockey players today are not a patch on the hockey players of yesteryear. Players back then had been hard, tough and underpaid – not at all like the whining sissies of the present age. In the image of these old warriors, Burke had his hair almost totally removed every two weeks by a barber whose business came mostly from a nearby army base.

Burke's being awake when so many slept was the current manifestation of his iron-willed leadership. It was taking immense will power and no end of black coffee, but he was awake and he was worrying. Faced with discipline of this magnitude, sleep did not stand a chance.

On the other side of the cabin, a couple of rows farther to the rear, centre Dougie Burns and left-winger Smitty Smith were awake in their adjoining seats. Smitty's being so was remarkable. As a rule, he conked out on the runway and had to be bludgeoned awake for meals. He was awake now only because of the behaviour of Burns, his linemate, roommate and best friend.

Each time Smith would doze, Burns rattled the pages of the *Spectator* in his ear. "I've had it, Smitty. I'm not taking it anymore." On the *Spectator*'s sports page, Burns had angrily circled portions of Pop Gunn's column. "Listen to this shit. 'As usual when the Bisons are skating through molasses and losing every game, much of the blame can be settled on the shrugging shoulders of overpaid Doug Burns.' That's crap, Smitty. I'm not the least bit overpaid."

"I know, Dougie, but like I'm really...."

"And here, get the ending. 'If this team doesn't unload the likes of floater Doug Burns, there will be a large-scale fan revolt. Mark my prophetic words.' Somebody should mark that old fool's words with a big red pencil."

One other passenger was awake on Flight 941 but, unlike the others, this one was pretending to be asleep. In the window seat a row behind Smith and Burns, a bloated young man in a dusty black suit lay with a little pillow between his head and the oval window frame. The eyes were shut, the mouth was slack, the jaws were blue-black with coming beard. It was as convincing a sham of sleep as you're ever apt to see and the only giveaway, requiring a parallel view down his empty row, was the fact that the young man's fingers would occasionally do a dance over the keyboard of the laptop computer flipped open before him. This was Suds Saperstein, hockey columnist for the Bisons' home city tabloid and Pop Gunn's only rival.

Over the next hour, the final beacons winked out. Smitty, the first to go, announced his change of state with horselike snores. Burns, who had gone to sleep so often to this serenade, succumbed to it again. Captain Burke fell asleep with his eyes wide open, a sleep tortured by dreams of brush-cut warriors skating hard and hurling themselves against the end boards for no reason. Coach Wad's head fell forward on the final approach to slumber. Humorous diversion for the steward and stewardesses, the coach's straw had popped out from behind his jacket lapel and probed neatly up one hairy nostril. He would jerk back without waking, then slowly descend onto the straw again.

15

Satisfied that no hockey-interested person could observe him now, Saperstein bobbed up from his pillow and waved wildly to the stewardess for coffee. He began to type.

"Pop Gunn's crystal ball is flickering again these days and, in amongst its interior clouds, Pop thinks he spies a Bisons shakeup and a fan revolt...."

It is worth mentioning that, at this exact moment, Pop Gunn began having his French fry dream: a recurring dream in which Pop is pelted from a white fluorescent sky by sizzling *pommes frites*.

To understand the relationship between Pop Gunn and Suds Saperstein, it is necessary to go back, far back, to the time before the NHL Bisons moved north to their present home city in Western Canada. The Bisons were no more than a mote in local millionaire Angus Topworth's eye when Pop Gunn, already the veteran of the *Spectator*'s sportswriting staff, wrote his first prediction as regards them.

"This city *will have* its long-awaited, long-deserved NHL franchise," Pop wrote one spring day. "What's more, this franchise will come to town within twenty-four months." And then, for some reason unbeknownst perhaps to Pop himself, he added, "Mark my prophetic words."

Pop had been covering hockey for the *Spectator* for many years, everything from peewee up to the city's top attraction, the Junior A Chinooks. The city had always been interested in an NHL franchise, it was certainly hockey-mad enough, but every attempt in that direction had been foiled – you could even say "scorned" – by the league's governors and team owners. The city, a Western Canadian prairie city, was seen as simply too rustic for the "Bigs," a backwater with zero television appeal in Eastern Canada and south of the border. Pop had expended thousands of words on the unfairness of this, the downright Eastern snootiness of it all.

But Pop's prediction of an NHL franchise for the city, far-fetched as it seemed at the time when it was written, did come true, and within the two-year time limit. A failing franchise, wilting in the heat of a southern U.S. city, was threatening to fold. Its attractiveness to favoured American purchasers had been dealt a severe blow by a well-circulated, also well-founded, rumour of cocaine abuse among the players. Multi-millionaire Angus Topworth stepped in at the last minute with a bid to move the team to Western Canada. Because his was the only offer, it was grudgingly accepted. The team, redubbed the Bisons, came to Pop Gunn's prairie city.

The successful prediction made a local hero of Pop, as if he'd had a direct hand in bringing the team to town. What he'd in fact had was a few drinks with prospective owner Topworth but Pop himself seemed to have forgotten that. Praised in his own town and called upon increasingly to discuss the new franchise for the likes of the CBC and *Maclean's*, Pop's sense of his own importance puffed up, as did his faith in his ability to read the team's collective palm. In the Bisons's first few months of existence, Pop went on a predicting rampage, always concluding such columns with the trademark sentence:

"Mark my prophetic words."

Around this time, the Bisons acquired their first general manager, a much-travelled ex-player who had earned himself the nickname Dealer Dan. Arriving in Bisontown, Dealer Dan Rapelli promised a rapid-fire reshuffle of Bison player cards; he promised a winning deck in just the Bisons's second year. Pop's litany of forecasts made in response to those of Dealer Dan featured the following:

Dealer Dan would indeed make several quick trades.

Not one of the players linked to drugs in the old city would see ice-time in a Bisons uniform.

As a result of Dealer Dan's trades, the Bisons would finish dead last in the NHL in their first two seasons.

If it was good news that the last-place finishes would allow the Bisons to draft first the following two springs, the more than offsetting bad news was that Dealer Dan would by then have traded these first-round picks to other teams.

The pointlessness of these early trades would eventually cost Dealer Dan his job. Mark Pop's prophetic words.

And it all came true.

Superstitious as sports fans generally are, none saw anything occult in Pop's ability to foretell the future. Rather, he was seen as a shrewd hockey analyst, plunking the right variables in the right equations and, hence, being able to write the news in advance. Desire to get the news before it occurred led to a terrific boom in sales for the *Spectator* at exactly the time when a new tabloid in town was trying to establish itself as a threat to the older paper's circulation. After Dealer Dan made his predestined exit from town, there was even a local petition to have Pop take his place. Though Pop was never employed directly by the Bisons, it was rumoured that team owner Topworth often invited him to have lunch at his club.

It was truly the golden age of Pop's career, blessed with the kind of respectability and power that most sportswriters only dream of. It fit Pop's reputation beautifully that, far from seeming delighted with his success, the old man looked, if anything, grumpier. What wasn't generally known was that Pop looked grumpier because *he was grumpier*.

For starters, Pop hated the news he was writing so accurately in advance. Locked in the cellar by Christmas in years one and two, the Bisons were a kind of charming joke. When they got the same death grip on last place by Yuletide of year three, they were still a joke but the charm was gone. They were a terrible and inexplicably uninspired team. They had no stars and Dealer Dan's freedom with draft choices meant they were unlikely to get any for years to come.

Pop hated this hopelessness and, something less apparent, he also hated his ability to predict things. It wasn't something he had ever had before and it was not something that extended beyond the realm of the Bisons hockey team. Losses and debts incurred at thoroughbred race meets were ample evidence of that. This marking of prophetic words was new and spooky for Pop, nor could he seem to stop doing it. If some felt he had hold of the inner workings of Angus Topworth's and Dealer Dan's minds, Pop felt now that someone or something had hold of his. What if he should suddenly foresee a plane crashing while he was on it? And what the hell did the dream mean? Why was he always dreaming now about French fries flying down out of an electric sky?

Under the influence of these two powerful depressants, Pop's columns became ever grouchier, oscillating between banshee-shrill predictions of catastrophe and dark, brooding, almost Sartrelike, statements about the hopelessness and meaninglessness of hockey played in the Bisons's style.

If one were to read and analyze all of Pop's writings during this blue period, it would not be hard to isolate a central theme. Just as Eve and Adam had loused things up for mankind by having themselves evicted from paradise, Pop saw the Bisons's dependable failure as also having issued from a set of original sins. The number one draft choices Dealer Dan had long ago traded to the winds were flesh and blood now. Whereas number one drafts often don't pan out and become embarrassments to the drafting team, the two in a row that Dealer Dan traded away turned quickly into bona fide NHL stars. Both became franchise players for other teams.

The other half of this original sin package consisted of what Dealer Dan got in return for those drafts. Mostly he had traded for proven, experienced players (who turned out to be old, tired and somewhat beyond their prime). He also received a pair of draft choices near the end of the first round. Dealer Dan had used these to select a young centre named Doug Burns and a fighter named Rodney "Smitty" Smith.

No name turned up as often in Pop's column as that of Doug Burns. The drafting of Burns, "a natural scorer with more no-hitters to his credit than Nolan Ryan," Pop called "hare-brained in the extreme." The retaining of Burns, year after year, Pop called "sports masochism" and the "compounding of a massive blunder." Everything Pop hated about the Bisons was best symbolized by the arty but frightened playing style of Burns. When Pop turned his ray of rage on team players, it hit Burns first and then whomever was near enough to catch the splatter.

When Pop first predicted the coming of the Bisons, Suds Saperstein was thousands of kilometres away, a fat and pimpled teenager hanging around the sidedoors of Maple Leaf Gardens, eating hotdogs and trying to get Toronto players to sign his hockey cards. When the Bisons skated forth for their first NHL game, Saperstein was fatter still and had taken his obsession with the game of hockey to a Toronto college offering a diploma in sports journalism. The spring that Dealer Dan left Bisontown, Saperstein arrived to take up employment with the newly born tabloid, covering a few of the city's amateur sports leagues for a pittance. How such a one as this acquires within a few months his own column for coverage of an NHL team is a good question but one with a fairly simple answer.

Writing his memoirs on some future day, Suds Saperstein will credit his boundless determination and his emulation of the fair and not-so-fair tactics of his most tenacious hockey heros. All this will be lies and nonsense. Suds Saperstein got the job of covering the Bisons because no one else wanted it. When one newspaper (the *Spectator*) can trace its considerable success to the popularity of one column (Pop's), the corresponding column in the rival and failing newspaper (the *Orb*) becomes a dangerous thing to write. In short, the *Orb*'s hockey column was a graveyard, one in which a couple of fairly decent careers had already been laid to rest. Even at that Suds had to beg for his chance and all he was given was the games up until Christmas to show a dramatic increase in readers.

To cut the story short as possible, Saperstein tried all sorts of things to build his audience but, conducting his own secret telephone survey in mid-October, he discovered he was getting nowhere. Several of those he phoned praised Pop Gunn as an honest guy, a guy who got things right, a guy who could be depended on for the straight poop. Why should they read anyone else?

Not surprisingly Saperstein developed an obsession with Pop Gunn. He tried to talk to the old man in the press box and to approach him on the concourse between periods but Pop generally acted as if he weren't there. Sometimes, when Pop was in his cups, he would suddenly gain the ability to see and hear Saperstein but only for purposes of ridicule. Turning from chit-chat with his TV and radio cronies, the old man might say, "The *Orb*, that what you work for? That's that yellow thing with the naked girl in it, right? I think I saw it in an outhouse once with the front page ripped off." When he got his laugh, he would again omit Suds from the range of things he could perceive.

On his own time Saperstein began reading his way backward through Pop's columns. He had only planned to read a couple of months' worth but again obsession seized him. He went to the *Spectator*'s gloomy old morgue and, photocopying as he went, extended his research back through the years.

From end to end of the freezing bed sitter which was all Saperstein could afford, piles of Pop's columns became the principal furniture. They lay in roughly chronological piles. His hopes a ruin, his meagre income translating into rent and beer, Suds would crawl among the piles, pushing away take-out boxes and his own soiled underwear, rereading bits and pieces of Pop's angry prophecies. He was looking for something. That's what he told himself. He was looking for something and, even though he did not know what it was, this looking was the only order that remained in his life.

When Suds actually found the thing he was looking for, he had more or less ceased to look. The truth was he was very drunk at the time. Having consumed a flat of twenty-four canned beer, he was lying face down on the carpet of paper debating the merits of a self-induced vomit. He opened a bloodshot eye hoping to jam the helicopter propeller in his head and directly in front of the eye were the words, "Burns will not...."

Seized with anger, Saperstein grabbed the page and sat up. "What the hell won't Burns do?" he shouted at the page and again at the naked walls. "Burns will not be offered another contract to play for the Bisons. Not even this organization could be that stupid. Mark my prophetic words."

Suddenly, Saperstein's nausea was gone. He was running on his knees to the filing cabinet, jerking open the bottom drawer. He pawed through a folder of his own columns and found a training camp ditty that read: "It's hard to know who's been holding out on whom but Doug Burns's contract situation was resolved yesterday. The three-year veteran signed a two-year pact with the Bisons. A lot of people don't like Burns but, let's face it, folks, he's still the only Bison to ever score thirty while wearing the uniform. Someone's got to put the puck in the net for this team."

Suds held the two columns up side by side. He bestowed beery kisses on both of them.

POP FIRES BLANK

My fellow scribe at the *Spectator*, the venerable Pop Gunn, likes to predict what's coming down the pipe for our hockey Bisons. He's pretty good at it too. But having looked through Pop's opus of previous years, I've discovered that Pop has made a booboo or two.

Listen to this from a couple of years ago: "Burns will not be offered another contract to play for the Bisons. Not even this organization could be that stupid. Mark my prophetic words."

Well, I'm marking them, all right, Pop, but what was that the Bisons offered Dougie this summer that he signed? I suspect it was a contract because Burns is certainly playing for the local side again this year, leading the team in goals as usual.

Not only is Dougie playing for the Bisons, he has never missed a Bisons game and handily owns the franchise's Iron Man record in this city. Got a comment, Pop? I'll be watching for it.

The magic of an inspired idea comes not from suspecting it might work; it comes from the absolute certainty that the machinery involved must churn in the direction that will make it work. Suds wrote his column and waited smugly for what he knew would come next. And it did: Pop Gunn's outraged reply in the *Spectator*. Just like clockwork, Pop hauled out the biggest guns in his arsenal and, sounding exactly like a lunatic, let fly.

"A pimply kid with no experience thinks... taking perfectly reasonable statements out of context ... libelous attack ... cheap attention-getting...."

When Suds' boss came in holding Pop's column and wanting Suds to respond, recant, disclaim, Suds said no, not yet. Only when Pop finally directed his column at another subject did Suds return to his theme.

It seems that something said in this column has got a rival sportswriter's old goat.

Like many of you, I am quite an admirer of Pop Gunn. To go on for decades despite infirmity: it's quite a symbol for a young sports scribe.

But also I have to say that nothing in Pop's several rebuttals changes the facts: Pop said the Bisons would never give Burns another contract and they have. End of sermon.

And, while we're at it, I found something else Pop wrote a long while back, another possible case of fog in the old crystal ball.

"The Bisons can't hope to have a winning team until year five," sayeth Pop. This is good news, folks. Here we are in year five and, though you'd never think so by the way they're playing, the Bisons are about to go on a tear.

They're about to win thirty of their next forty games! If they happen not to, you might give Pop a call and ask exactly what he meant by *winning season* and *year five*.

Could be that I'm taking his words out of context again.

After Suds filed this column, he went to see his boss. "I was wondering if I was still on probation around here," he said. "If so maybe I better start looking for more secure employment." The *Orb* had been selling a lot more copies since Suds had started his war with Pop. Both Suds and his boss knew it. The boss made a bowing gesture, like a man bending himself over a barrel. He offered Suds a significant raise. A desk closer to the window and a budget for travelling to road games were soon forthcoming.

Pop felt like his head was in a vice. On the back, the pressure came from Suds Saperstein who, by some awful coincidence, was sitting two rows behind him in the Montreal Forum press box. The junky tabloid he wrote for had never before found the coin to send its hockey hack on the road. Pop didn't like any of the possible meanings of this development.

The other half of the head-vice was that fairy Doug Burns, pirouetting around like some kind of figure skater in the pregame skate. In his high nasal voice, Saperstein yelled, "Go get 'em, Dougie!" It was an absurd thing for a reporter in a press box to do but even stranger was the fact that Burns acted as if he heard the voice. He chose that time to look up in their direction, to raise a hand and wave.

Pop's vision went dark, as if a cloud had passed before the sun. His head pulsed against his normally comfortable hat band. He had visions of the African tall grass plains, of an old lion that had once ridden speedy gazelles to the ground being alternatively bled and starved to death by a mosquito on his back and a tapeworm up his....

The crowd cheered lustily and only then did Pop realize that he had missed both the national anthem and the opening face-off. He sat forward and tried to concentrate. That idiot Chip Wad had started the Burns line again. Burns had lost the face-off – is the Pope Catholic – and within a minute a Montreal winger broke in alone behind the Bisons defence and parked the puck casually behind Carrasco. All around Pop, the Forum fans jumped up to bestow French blessings on their heros. Inside himself, Pop was screaming at least as loud. Why, he bayed, why won't anyone listen to me? If the Bisons head office had ever behaved with an ounce of sense, Burns would have been gone after the first season. He might have had a shred of trade value back then. The contract prediction had been a good prediction. It should have come true.

Pop remembered the last game before they left on this road trip, how Burns had caused his team to do something Pop had never seen at any level of hockey above peewee. A line came off the ice and no one had gone on. Burns and his idiotic linemates whose shift it was, and the defence pair too, had simply sat there like so many potted plants while Pop from his honoured place had screamed, "Why? Why?" at the bent back of Coach and General Manager Wad.

If Burns had been traded back then, it was entirely possible that the Bisons could have built a winning team by now. Year five could have been their first winning season. That too had been a good prediction.

The game in Montreal wore on. A ridiculously one-sided affair. Heaped onto Pop's head were two further irritations.

Burns scored twice, both flukes, and Saperstein dared approach Pop on the concourse between the second period and the third.

"Well, Pop, looks like you could be right about that shake-up."

Suds spoke these words then plugged his mouth with a relish-swollen hot dog. Pop imagined shoving the whole thing into the idiot's blubbery face, napkin and all, then holding the lips and nose shut until he suffocated. He also searched his mind for some piece of devastating sarcasm but his upstairs hallway was full of echoes.

"Sorry, maybe you've forgotten who I am. Saperstein of the *Orb*."

Pop looked at the hand Saperstein was pushing out at him. It was small and weak, all out of proportion to the body attached to it. Pop narrowly resisted an urge to spit in it. "Excuse me, I've got work to do," was all he could say.

"Keep up the predictions, Pop."

Pop went straight to the can. Standing at one of a long row of urinals, he couldn't pee. But if he didn't pee, he'd need to badly as soon as he sat down. He locked himself into a toilet cubicle and sat.

During the third period, Pop could not shake the feeling of imminent defeat. The Bisons, of course, were losing by a ton but that wasn't the kind of defeat Pop meant. It was personal defeat he feared. This kind of game would make any reasonable general manager demote half his squad, start all over again with foreigners and guys from the AHL. But before his mind's eye, Pop saw an unchanging roster. Another prediction in trouble. Another opening for that hyena, that slough leech Saperstein. And the worst thing was that Pop felt his clairvoyance had only deserted him in the realm of hockey. The French fries were still flying in his dreams. Last night on the plane there'd even been a burger.

Was this it then? The end of the line?

Just then another roar went up and the sound wasn't the sound that another Montreal goal would have prompted. It was the blood sound this time, the fight sound. Pop rose up in his seat to watch. On one side of the ice, the trainer was bent over a prostrate Montreal player. On the other side, a mixture of

Canadiens and Bisons was milling tightly around. When the benches cleared, Pop's mood began to improve. Nothing like a bench-clearing brawl to take the mind off unpleasantness.

But inevitably Doug Burns caught Pop's eye. Of course, he wasn't fighting. He hadn't even tied up another player, which was the accepted thing the wimps did to each other while others battled for real. Burns stood all alone, looking half asleep and – this was the worst – the candy ass was smiling.

But what's this? A young Canadien, tough and ugly, broke loose from the main scrum. He was flying toward Burns. Maybe he'd seen the smile too, thought Pop, seen it and taken it personally. The kid was grabbing Burns by the shoulders, wrenching him around, trying to pull his hockey sweater over his head. Then, oh joy, he was driving the top of his hockey helmet into Burns's mouth. With something approaching bliss, Pop watched Burns begin to bleed. He watched a white tooth emerge from Burns's lips. He watched it fall and bounce on the ice.

When the trainer skated Burns off the ice and down the ramp to the dressing room, Pop sat back down. He poised his fingers above the keyboard of his laptop computer. The gazelles were running; the old lion was up and rumbling to a gallop, steadily closing the helpless distance.

CALLING ALL BETTERS

Most players in this league wouldn't miss a shift over a busted tooth. For that matter, most juniors wouldn't either. Last night, in the third period of the Bisons's humiliation at the hands of the Montreal Canadiens, Doug Burns was parted from one of his pearly whites during a bench-clearing brawl. Burns was gone for the night. It was exactly what this reporter would have expected.

What's more, I'm willing to bet with anyone who reads this column that Burns does not play in Monday's matchup with the Rangers in New York.

That's right, readers, I'm putting my money where my mouth is that the consecutive games streak of this beer can Iron Man is over. In fact, though I won't actually predict it, I wouldn't be surprised if Burns hangs up his skates for good over this minor mishap.

> As for his missing the Monday game, count on it. Mark
> my prophetic words.

The game against the Canadiens in which Burns lost his tooth was on a Saturday. Thanks to the time zone difference and the miracle of modem, Pop's challenge to the betters of the nation made it into the Sunday morning *Spectator*. Realizing that potential takers would not be able to find him, Pop ran up his telephone credit card calling everybody on the continent with whom he had ever had a bet. He didn't get as much action as he had hoped. He could tell that people thought it a senseless thing to bet on, that they really did not care if Burns played the next game or not. But Pop continued to bully people into little five and ten dollar wagers anyway. Each bet, no matter how small or half-hearted, added to the drama in Pop's head, added to the glamour of his inevitable victory.

Saperstein spent Sunday morning, before the flight to New York, trying to find Burns. He'd had a clairvoyant little instinct of his own that Pop would make something of the fight and the lost tooth. He'd phoned back to Bisontown as soon as the first newspaper boxes there were filled and he'd got the precise wording of Pop's column. He'd phoned Burns's room to tell him, had searched the hotel coffee shop, had gone to the room and knocked. No answer. Finally, he'd slipped a transcription of the column under Burns's hotel room door with the following note attached: "Pop Gunn's column this morning. Crap. Let's prove him wrong. Your friend, Suds Saperstein of the *Orb*." But he had the feeling that Burns was not on the other side of that door.

Getting on the plane to New York, Suds had no opportunity to speak to Burns. From his seat at the back of the plane, he studied the young centre nonstop as the plane made its little arc to the Big Apple. Once in a while he would see Burns's hand go up in the direction of his lips. When the stewardess came to Burns's seat about lunch, he looked like he was covering his mouth entirely with his hand and speaking through the fingers. Saperstein passed up another copy of Pop's column and another note from himself, but all that happened was that Smitty Smith put it on Burns's untouched food tray and it went away with the stewardess a couple of minutes later.

In New York that afternoon, the Bisons had a compulsory practice. Burns was there but in his street clothes on the bench. He stared at the ice but his head didn't move side to side with the play. He kept touching his mouth. Pop was at the practice too but also never seemed to look at it. Whenever Suds glanced over, Pop was looking at a steno pad in his lap. When he applied his pen to it, it didn't look like writing, more like adding.

After the practice, there was a team meeting, closed to the press, and Saperstein went back to his hotel. He set out his laptop, sat down before its keyboard and little crystal screen. He knew what he was about to do; he knew it was a terrible mistake; he knew he would do it anyway.

Never a slow worker, Suds broke all previous records for speed in writing his next day's column. Though convinced that Pop was right, he wrote down that Pop was wrong and that Burns would surely play in Monday's game. Using Poplike language, he attacked Pop directly for even suggesting that Burns lacked the courage, the heart to play. Pop had gone too far this time and Doug Burns was about to prove it. Saperstein ended the piece: "Let's face it, folks, Pop Gunn couldn't predict a horse race at a merry-go-round."

But even as Saperstein sent the missive electronically home, in lots of time for the Monday morning edition, he knew who was the one going too far, the one acting really loony. The wild dice was cast and, through no fault but Suds's own, his career was retrieved from safety and set back into precarious balance.

A lot of people slept badly that night. Saperstein, who always overate, overate more than usual and spent the night waking up to boiling heartburn at the base of his throat and all the way down beneath his sternum. In Pop's dreams the burger was still present among the French fries and, when it woke him, he experienced disappointment as well as fear. He had hoped his resurgence as a lion rampant would vanquish the dream.

Steve Burke had a dream about his father in which his

father's hair was inexplicably draped over the tops of his ears. When he focused more closely on the manly lobe of his father's manly ear, he saw to his horror a diamond stud.

Doug Burns dreamt that he was at a party and had caught the eye of a beautiful woman. She was manoeuvring toward him, favouring him with smiles. He was edging away, trying to look natural while keeping his lips tightly shut. She caught up to him and asked him several witty and intelligent questions; he couldn't bring himself to speak. The warmth began to fade from her. But he dared not open his mouth.

The next night at Madison Square Garden, Suds waited in a shadow until Pop arrived by cab. Suds followed him at a distance and a good thing too because Pop did not go to the Garden press box. Instead, he bought himself a seat a few rows directly behind the Bisons bench, probably so that he could have a better view of the team's arrival. Once Pop was seated, Saperstein got himself a big snack and then returned toward Pop's place in the stands. The guard at the entrance to the section was occupied with a drunk and Saperstein easily got by. Then he was standing on the step above Pop's aisle seat, looking almost directly down on the crown of the old green fedora.

By now, Suds was convinced that Burns would not play, that Pop would win his bet as well as the battle of the hockey scribes. Suds was here because of some need to be close to Pop when all was revealed. Other than that he did not know what he intended. He saw himself congratulating Pop on his successful prediction then drifting quietly away. He also saw himself setting down his food and knitting his fingers tightly around Pop's swollen neck. What Suds did do was nothing, except watch as the Bisons filed out from under the canopy to the insane negative thunder of the New York fans.

As Suds expected, Burns was not there. The last yellow-helmeted head emerged and it did not belong to Burns. In front of Suds, Pop began to chuckle. The mass of flesh from his chin to his waist began to jump up and down in time. Saperstein bent down near the old man's ear and whispered, "Pop." He had to say it several times, each time louder, before the fedora began to turn.

Exactly as Pop's fedora completed its 180 degree turn, Doug Burns came out from under the canopy and began to skate tiredly across the ice. Burns was staring through a huge plastic visor, the fitting of which had kept him in the dressing room a little longer than the others. Pop did not see this because he was turned from the ice. Suds did see Burns and responded by gathering his bulk for a mighty victory leap.

Up Suds went, actually making it a few inches off the cement step. When he stopped going up and started coming down, his French fries left their paper container. When he crashed down, the impact jarred the burger loose from his hand, caused it to flip up among the falling fries.

While this was going on, Pop was trying to figure out who had been calling his name. What he saw first when he turned were the baggy knees of a huge pair of black trousers. Then the knees and all the rest began to go up, to rise off the ground. Raising his chin and peering beyond the front edge of his fedora brim, Pop was blinded for a second by the Gardens ceiling lights. Then from that white glare, the first of the French fries came. From that white sky, a burger was born, parting ways with itself, shedding both relish and onions.

Some stories end with a blaze of clarity where all is suddenly known. Other stories end in the opposite way: things that seemed clear turn foggy, even bizarre. This story is of the latter kind.

To this day, it is not known if what Pop had that night was a stroke, a heart attack, both or neither. Whatever it was that sent Pop sliding from his Madison Square Gardens seat also put him in a coma for eight solid days. The media back in Bison-town had Pop thoroughly praised, mourned and all but buried when the old trooper suddenly sat up in his New York City hospital bed, demanding a drink and a smoke, and a damn good explanation. He seemed all right to the doctors and, given American medical costs, no one put up much of an argument when he dressed and left for home.

Given the timing of his collapse, Pop arrived home still not knowing that Burns had played the New York game. Everyone was afraid to mention it for fear of bringing on a relapse. Certainly none of the people Pop had bets with wanted to collect. It is said that Pop found out only when he himself tried to collect from someone too miserly to lie.

Here the story gets very murky indeed. Apprised of the failed prediction and the umpteen lost bets, Pop did not do any of the things that past performance suggested he would do. No railing, no ranting, no attempt to dispute the facts. Burns, after all, had only played long enough to lose the opening face-off. He had skated from there to the bench complaining of head pain. Pop could have made a case, perhaps.

But the old lion did not roar at all; eye witnesses say he even smiled a bit when he said, "Oh well. Can't win 'em all."

An explanation for this? Sorry. It is simply not known why. Friends of Pop will tell you that, prior to his seizure, coma and recovery, he had been complaining a great deal about inability to sleep properly; they will tell you that, after his recovery, he complained of this not at all. Avid watchers of Pop's hockey column will tell you another two things: Pop never mentioned Doug Burns on the *Spectator* sports page again, starting the day he got back from hospital in New York, and he never again invited anyone to mark his prophetic words.

Also unknown to this ending is whether Burns played his minute of that game in New York to spite Pop. When asked about it, Burns claimed he had no idea what people were talking about – which might be the truth. Smitty Smith, Burns's roomie on the road, once said he doubted Burns even saw the column in question. After losing his tooth, Burns had gone into a kind of coma of his own, a waking kind, which is really part of another story to be told another time.

Suds Saperstein, in his memoirs, would claim that Burns had indeed acted to spite Pop and that, what's more, he had done so as a result of a challenge from Saperstein: Saperstein's having told him to stick up for himself, to show what he was really made of, etcetera. Don't bother trying to look up that one, though. The book hasn't been written yet and, when it has, what publisher is apt to be interested in an unknown reporter's half-season of covering a last place team?

Suds Saperstein's experiment with Poplike rhetoric

backfired in a totally unexpected way. His debunking of Pop and his accurate prediction that Burns *would* play didn't appear in the *Orb* the morning before the New York game. By some quirk of fate, or some editorial malfunction, it appeared the morning after. That is, it appeared in the *Orb* on Tuesday: the same morning that the *Spectator*'s front-page story was Pop's tragic fall in the aisles of Madison Square Garden. Not only was Saperstein's column a prediction after the fact, it was a sadistic kicking of a man while down.

People showed their rage at Saperstein in a variety of ways, including subscription cancellation, and Saperstein was notified of his firing in a St. Louis hotel on the last leg of his only road trip. Like Pop, he took his bad news with uncharacteristic calm. When he'd written the column that turned around to slay him, he had felt he was writing his own doom, and he'd been right. He had simply misunderstood the mechanism by which that doom would come.

As for Doug Burns, he received credit for the minute he played in New York against the Rangers and, given that he played every other game of that season, his Bisons Iron Man record was upped to three hundred and twenty straight games. It was a record that would take many years to fall.

Place of Pain

Two weeks after losing his first tooth to the game of hockey, Doug Burns realized that this was the worst thing that had ever happened to him. He was far from happy with his life but still, losing a tooth, his left front tooth, was the worst. It also came to him that he must correct this disfigurement and get on with the extensive menu of his other problems. Thus Burns entered the offices of Dr. Dent; thus he was introduced to the sultan's tent atmosphere of this supposed place of pain.

I lost my first tooth to the game of hockey in Montreal. After that, there were two more games on the road. Then came the longest home stand of the season. Usually teams look forward to that: being with their families, getting a feel for awhile of what it is like to have a home, watching your own TV. The guys who have wives and children make a huge sentimental deal of it, going to the zoo, the museum and every other thing. Somebody always gets the idea of staging a family skating party for the whole organization.

But this year, given the kind of losing streak we were on, even the husbands and fathers were dreading the home stand. It promised extra practices and endless team meetings. There would be trade rumours and the press would be around like so many vultures, looking for a morsel they might stretch into a meal. The fans were bound to boo and throw things.

What it promised for me personally, though, was dental work. The long stretch at home was my best chance to plug the gap in my smile, to correct (or disguise) the ugly disfigurement that was surprising me in the mirror every morning. I was at this time looking desperately for a wife and I couldn't look at any woman without clamping my mouth shut, without seeing the spectre of my dead tooth swimming in the air between us. In that sense I was probably the only one on the team looking forward to being home.

But there was a complication. My dentist and I had had a falling out.

I had been going to Dr. Bismark ever since I came to Bisontown as a rookie. He had over the years done what I expected any dentist of mine to do: nothing. My teeth were my pride. I had given them everything teeth and gums could want: brushing, flossing, fluoride. I went to Dr. Bismark every six months for a modest cleaning, the little bit of plaque removal that my own flossing had missed, but mainly to hear the words, "Perfect, Doug. Your teeth are perfect."

Dr. Bismark had never failed me in this regard until my last checkup, eight months before I lost the tooth in Montreal. It had been in the spring after the end of the previous hockey season and he had said that perhaps an X-ray was in order. He seldom did these on me, so confident was he in the perfection of my teeth. But he did one that day and, holding the black-grey plastic up to the light, he winced and said, "Oooh."

"What do you mean, oooh?"

"See here, Doug? It's what I've been fearing for some time."

"Wait a minute. What's this fearing? You said my teeth were perfect."

At that moment my whole opinion of Dr. Bismark changed,

even my visual image of him. I saw that his glasses were not clean. They had stuff, maybe dandruff, on them. Dandruff. His dandruff had been falling in my mouth while he went the rounds with his mirror and pick.

"I didn't want to alarm you, Doug. I thought it might turn on its own but it hasn't."

His examining room was tacky in the extreme. The chair I was reclined in was a sickly green. The dental health posters on the walls hadn't been changed in years. The one across from me was ripped on one corner, an ear of paper hanging down. "What might turn?"

"Your wisdom tooth, Doug."

"There's not a thing wrong with my wisdom teeth."

I said this not without realizing what a vast thing it was for a patient to say to a dentist who was looking at his X-ray.

"But, see here, Doug. I'll admit the three of your wisdom teeth that have erupted are beautiful teeth, very healthy for wisdom teeth, but this one, see?"

I looked where he was pointing. At the end of the lower left-hand row of molars, within the gum, there was something strange which I hated to believe was mine. It was a fully formed tooth, molar in construction, and it was lying on its side, its fat end poised like a battering ram a small distance from the root of the next tooth. Bismark was continuing to speak.

"The tooth is impacted, Doug. It will never erupt on its own. When the crown hits the root of the next tooth, it will damage it, maybe even kill it. And back here, the root is dangerously close to a facial nerve. If it strikes that nerve, all hell could break loose. It could effect your speech. It must be surgically removed, Doug."

"Why didn't you tell me this before?"

"In rare cases, such a tooth will change direction and erupt properly. I knew how much your teeth meant to you, I knew how alarmed you would be...."

"I'm alarmed now!" I fear I was yelling. Dr. Bismark's elderly dental assistant's face appeared from around the corner, wearing a look of great concern.

"Where are you going, Doug?"

For I had indeed jumped up from the reclined chair. I had

ripped the paper thing from around my neck, had balled it up and thrown it on the floor.

"To another dentist, that's where!"

But it was a lie. I didn't go to another dentist and, as bad or worse, I began neglecting my teeth. Oh, I brushed and flossed but not with the old vigour and not on the old rigid schedule. Days sometimes passed without a single strand of floss between my teeth.

I realize now I was in a state of denial. Because I could not change Dr. Bismark's sentence, I denied it. I carried on as if this sideways molar in my gum wasn't there or belonged to someone else. A sort of spring-loaded barrier existed in my mind. If my thoughts or a conversation began to head down the neurological highway in a dental direction, the barrier automatically sprang up, cutting off access.

That is, it remained so until the lout in Montreal smashed out my tooth with his helmet. The shock did something besides remove a front tooth; it also jimmied the barrier apparatus and I knew in that instant that a new dentist must be found and obeyed.

But who would this new dentist be? Surprisingly, I had an idea of someone to try. During my period of denial, one of the things I had ignored (but retained subconsciously) was a diatribe on dentistry from our team captain, Steve Burke. Burke had had a few more of his teeth smashed early in the season, which for him rated in severity about as high as jock itch. He had tried out a new dentist named Dr. Dent and he hadn't been impressed.

"He was afraid," was Steve's assessment. "It was like I came to him with my arm ripped off." Dr. Dent had suggested that Burke must be in a lot of pain. "Try a shoulder separation if you want pain, I told him. A torn up knee ligament, that'll give you pain." Dr. Dent offered Burke laughing gas but Burke was against mind or mood-altering substances.

"Come on, Doc," he'd said, "just get in there with the pliers, rip out the splinters and get it over with."

Finally Dr. Dent was simply too hesitant; Burke dumped him for a more old-fashioned dentist of the extraction-by-force school.

Driven out of my state of denial, I remembered this conversation. I remembered the name Dr. Dent.

Dr. Dent's office requires description. Entering from a perfectly ordinary office complex corridor, I felt enveloped by something. I wondered if he snuck a little laughing gas into his air-conditioning system. The waiting room was certainly filled with laughter.

A great many women in white, behind desks and walking around, all smiling and all attractive, took me over the instant I came in. One took my coat and ushered me to a desk. Behind that desk another inquired about the nature of my difficulty. A third woman behind a second desk asked how I was intending to pay. She gently lifted my team dental insurance card from my fingers and said that was absolutely all she needed. She conveyed me to a huge and soft armchair and placed that month's *Sports Illustrated* in my hands, opened to an article about hockey.

As I pretended to read, the chuckling continued, hearty badinage between the women interrupted by occasional phone calls in – or out to patients whose names had surfaced on the computer. "Hello, Mr. Kingfisher. It's Emily at Dr. Dent's office. It's over six months since your last appointment. You really should come in for a cleaning. Is there any problem with your insurance? You know that Dr. Dent would be happy to accept a postdated cheque."

Then from the inner chambers came a patient, a lady with that look you get after a dental appointment, the anxiety occasioned by belief that you are slobbering and that your face is twice its normal size. One of the smiling staff asked if she needed a taxi, another bundled her into her winter coat and eased her out the door.

Then out came another smiling female employee, not in

white but in a kind of bluey-green uniform. It was, for me, the colour of the Mediterranean on a sunny day. She walked out of the back and into my heart. She said, "Doug?" And I said, "Yes." And she said, "All set to come in?" And I said, "Oh, yes."

And I jumped up, really sprang up, and trotted at her heels down a hallway. We passed a maze of cubicals with dental chairs, some occupied, until she led me into her own alcove, a tiny one at the rear with a chair the Mediterranean colour of her uniform. I sat and she reclined the chair. It was like a bed, one so comfortable I would have bought it on the spot to sleep in at home.

From above and behind, her face came looming like a rising sun. We were looking at each other's eyes upside-down which, as you know, can be a disconcerting, almost horror-movie sensation. The mind refuses to accept that the eyes are upside-down, insists on viewing them as if they were right-side-up, which puts the eyelashes and eyebrows on the wrong side. Anyway, it wasn't like that at all. Somehow, this woman's eyes managed to look perfect, hazel and symmetrical, kind but firm, no matter which way up they were.

"My name is Judy. I'm a dental technician. I'm going to clean your teeth."

But first she did an X-ray. Judy knew I was a hockey player. She said she didn't watch hockey much herself but that Dr. Dent was a great fan and was very proud that I had come to his clinic. I had noticed by now that all the women in the establishment had a special tone to their voice, almost reverent, when Dr. Dent's name was mentioned. Judy was the same and I found myself angrily jealous of the yet unseen Dr. Dent.

Judy had finished the X-ray by now. She probed about in my mouth with a hooked prong. She got a grip on something with the hook. She gave a powerful tug and something cracked. I thought she had broken another tooth in half. I would have forgiven her if she had.

"What was that?"

"Plaque."

The ugly word, and addressed to me. I felt great shame.

"You have a ridge below your gum line. Do you floss, Doug?"

Humiliated, I confessed that I had been recently lax with the floss.

"I can tell," she said. "I can tell both that you haven't been lately and, before that, you did."

She was really working me over now, raking at the gum line, changing instruments frequently, wiping blood on the napkin she had chained around my neck.

"What else can you tell?" I asked, deeply afraid.

She sniffed, a short sharp sniff through nostrils as clean as a whistle. "I can tell by the smell that the ridge line of plaque is causing a low-grade infection of the gum."

I couldn't help it. My mouth clamped shut, right on her dental instrument. She jiggled it, pried my mouth back open. She chuckled merrily. "Don't be embarrassed, Doug. Almost everyone has it to some degree. I smell it all the time and it doesn't bother me one little bit."

I confess it. That's when I fell in love with Judy, in that moment when she so graciously accepted my infected breath. After that, I lay back and rolled happily with the punches: the surprisingly violent war she was waging with my plaque; the elementary lecture on gum disease and flossing which, from anyone else, would have driven me mad with indignation. I had to ask her out, I knew this; and, if she were to accept that offer, I was also pretty sure I would ask her to marry me.

All too soon Judy was handing me on to Dr. Dent. The song in her voice when she said his name pried up a good-sized sod of resentment in me. Dent was sitting there in front of a white light with my X-ray hanging from a clip. He was a handsome sort, I guess, youthful and athletic-looking, smiling like everyone else around here. Judy seemed highly nervous when, in the presence of Dr. Dent, I spoke to her and not to him.

"Do you think I need another cleaning, Judy? The one you just gave me was great but I'm really concerned about that gum line infection."

Judy looked around me at Dr. Dent. I had a feeling he was nodding.

"Well, sure, Doug. I guess I could do more. When are you thinking of?"

"Right away. As soon as possible. While the team's in town."

Dr. Dent must have nodded again.

"Could we call you then, Doug? I'm all booked up but sometimes there are cancellations."

"That would be great, really great."

I shook her hand and she ran away. Keeping Dr. Dent waiting was evidently a big no-no. By the time I actually sat down, I had Dr. Dent pegged as a phoney, a closet tyrant, the kind who forced this all-in-the-family crap on his staff, subtly threatening them with unemployment were they to feel less than chuckley one day.

Once I was there beside him, Dr. Dent tried a bunch of sports talk on me. He claimed that his dream had been to be a professional hockey player. I told him it wasn't all it was cracked up to be; that, besides, he was probably too thin. I imagined him being hit by my cornerman Smitty Smith and snapping like a dry pretzel.

He went into the X-ray and, when I saw what direction his finger was pointing, I cut him off. "The wisdom tooth is impacted, I know that. What I want right now is an artificial front tooth. It may be vanity but that's what I want."

He didn't like hearing that but he finally conceded it was my mouth. We got onto talking about how, and how soon, my new tooth could be moulded, made and fitted in place. Thinking of Judy, I told him it couldn't be any too soon for me.

Later that week, Judy had a cancellation and I was literally waiting beside the phone when Dr. Dent's office called. Could I come in an hour? I could. I was supposed to be at practice but I phoned Chip the coach and told him I was having emergency dental surgery.

Soon Judy was up there above me again with the upside-down eyes, picking away at the last crumbs of plaque under my gum. She seemed frustrated by the little there was to do and I tried to ease her pain by asking earnest questions about how best to floss, about the validity of advertising claims by gargles and pastes that were supposed to eliminate the problem. Her fingers were bare of significant rings but I knew that, in her line of work, she could hardly wear them if she had them. Finally, sensing that my time was almost up, I gambled.

"Your husband must have great teeth," I said, laughing too loud.

"He would have," she said with a chuckle.

"Would have? I don't get it."

"If I had one."

"I guess what I mean is, women in your profession must find men with dental imperfections unattractive."

"Oh, I wouldn't say that. I'm sure some women in my profession wouldn't mind at all. Especially in a case like yours where the dental habits have been overall good and the lasting damage isn't your fault."

I tried to control myself but couldn't. Before another breath could be drawn by either of us, I had asked Judy out. Though evidently troubled by something, she said she supposed she could. I tried to recall my exact words. What had I invited her to do?

"Dinner then?" I hazarded.

"That would be all right."

For the last few minutes of my appointment, her probing in my mouth, her recitation of oral health tips, seemed moody and distant.

Dr. Dent became hostile toward me. Early in the following week, when he did the mould for my new tooth, he hardly chatted about hockey at all. When I asked if the tooth would be ready before my next road trip, he verged on nasty.

"You are not our only patient, Doug. In less than two weeks you've had two cleanings and two appointments with me. The manufacture of an artificial tooth is an art. You should be glad it can't be done overnight because, if it could, you wouldn't want the tooth."

Yes, I would, I thought. My dinner date with Judy was on Friday, the night before the team left for Winnipeg. I would

41

have paid a lot of money to wear any kind of tooth that night where currently I lacked one.

"What's your hurry?" asked Dent, and I believed right then, as certain as death, that he was aware of my date with Judy, aware and disapproving. My opinion of him plummeted again, until it had nowhere farther down to go. This harem of his. This carefully assembled coterie of attractive, ever-smiling women. He, the sheik, ruling their lives and facial expressions by financial blackmail. I would free Judy from the grasp of this sinister man. I would use all my money if necessary to buy her a good dentist with whom to work.

Unable to do anything about my tooth, I used the last days before our date to buy a new wardrobe and to clean my apartment as it had never been cleaned before. Given that it had hardly ever been cleaned before, this wasn't saying much, but I did, in fact, clean it very clean. I had no intention whatsoever of being so indecently importunate as to ask Judy to come to my apartment after dinner. But in the highly unlikely event that she suggested it, I wanted the place in mint condition. I even bought some new furniture.

The several suits of clothing were bought one per day. Between the time the stores closed one day and opened the next, my opinion of my latest outfit had declined to where I wouldn't have been buried in it. In the end I opted for an older suit that wives of my teammates had told me looked good. I also bought an arsenal of gargles, mouth washes, sprays and mints.

It didn't matter what I did, though, what I wore; right up to the moment I left to pick Judy up for dinner, all I could see in the mirror was my missing tooth, all I could smell was my mind's simulation of what gum line infection must smell like.

Judy lived in an apartment not far from Dr. Dent's office. She was waiting in the foyer and she got into the car just as I was leaping out to open her door. I'd had my Porsche hand-washed, waxed and vacuumed that day and her first comment was that

I had a nice car. I couldn't decide whether to show off the car's power or to give an impression of mature caution. As a result I drove both too fast and too slow, and gave the impression of being insane.

I took Judy to *Le Nuit*, an expensive French restaurant. It's food was reputed to be excellent but I had eaten there so often I didn't care for it anymore. The reason I'd ruined it for myself was in preparation for just such a night as tonight. I knew the menu backwards and forwards, I knew the staff, and I knew that, in movies at least, this kind of familiarity with a fine restaurant was a sure sign of sophistication.

Thus it was that I asked François what was special tonight and he said something in French which I translated for Judy as a recommendation of rabbit stewed in red wine with pearl onions. People can often look odd colours in candlelight but the green sheen on Judy's face right then was in truth green. She had to excuse herself for a moment which was more like ten. When she came back she was pale but composed. I made no more suggestions about the menu.

Often during that meal, I forgot to notice its silence. I would be looking at Judy, something I was convincing myself I could do for the rest of my life, and I would perhaps notice how a conversation at another table which had been about a recent holiday in Germany was now about the unfairness of law school admission tests. Though I was convinced our silence was that rare, comfortable kind so few couples enjoy, I decided as well that a little conversation couldn't hurt. At one point this led me to the subject of Dr. Dent.

All I said was, "What do you make of Dr. Dent?" But Judy's response was as if I had said, "Isn't that Dr. Dent a creep?" *What do you think of John Doe* is never a neutral question after all. It is asked because the asker has a strong opinion about him one way or the other. You can usually tell which. So Judy launched into a fervent defence of her boss.

Dr. Dent, she said, was a deeply caring man. She knew what people thought of dentists, and said about them, that they were all just in it for the money. But Dr. Dent wasn't like that at all. A patient's mouth was a precious thing to him. He hated to give pain. It hurt him, it really did. Did I know how high the suicide rate was for dentists? All his staff feared for Dr. Dent, feared for his very life, such was his personal agony over the slightest twinge he caused in others. And he was more than willing to take postdated cheques.

As far as Judy was concerned, I had had my say about Dr. Dent. When I tried to recant, tried to proclaim myself convinced that he really was a saint and a tragically suicidal victim of his own goodness, she paid no attention. I was so far gone that, when the Dr. Dent thing finally finished, my only conclusion was that I must accept Dr. Dent in order to live in harmony with Judy. With some people it is the father or the mother you must accept; with Judy it was Dr. Dent. Simple. So be it.

How sadly soon the meal was over. Judy said she was sorry that she had to go home but tomorrow was a work day and they started very early at Dr. Dent's. I paid the bill and we jumped back in the Porsche. I managed to open the door for her this time. Then it was her place and she was pointing her small strong hand at me. I knew this technique. It was a pre-emptive sort of thing designed to inform even the loutiest male that she did not wish to be approached by his lips. The real hosers invariably tried to kiss the hand.

I was deeply hurt by this development. The whole night began to unravel behind me like a sweater with a knitting flaw. The conversational lapses were comfortable no longer; they were iron silences, tension-filled. The discussion about Dr. Dent went from something I had accepted to something by which I had been rejected.

Well, so goes the cookie. What did I expect looking and smelling like I did? I took the opportunity, though, to ask a few vital questions.

"Judy, I need you to be very honest with me. Recognizing as I do that this date has failed and that you wish to go and not be called again, recognizing and respecting your choice, could I ask you if it's possible for you to be interested in a man missing a tooth?"

"No."

"Really? No?"

"Really no."

"You don't have to say that to ensure that I'll leave you alone. I promise to regardless of your opinion of my teeth."

"No."

"Why not?"

"I have a thing about teeth. The man I love will be a man with perfect teeth."

"I used to have perfect teeth."

"You don't now."

"But you said some women in your profession probably wouldn't mind at all."

"Some women in my profession probably wouldn't. It's just that I do. I know it's a character flaw. I know I shouldn't be so conscious of appearance. But I am. I'm being honest. Thank you for dinner, Doug."

"And if I had my artificial tooth it wouldn't make any difference."

"Not to me. I'm sure it will be a beautiful tooth. Good night."

"Good night, Judy."

I watched until Judy was inside. Doug, I said to myself in the confiding way I have with myself, your deepest fear about your missing tooth has just been confirmed in the worst possible way.

I pulled away from the curb and began the drive home. It was not far but I took it very slowly, taking the time to note things I would otherwise have overlooked: how sparks seemed to leap up from the snow under the cobra-headed lamps; how a low helmet of cloud was sealing in the city's light, making the giant furls of steam off the office towers glow.

Cars beeped at me on the four-lane that bent along the river; they swept around me at angry speed. "Hey, give me a break," I said aloud to them. "I'm having a life-changing moment, here."

As is my way with disasters, I was looking for a second perspective on the night's events and finally I found one. That is: if my most recent experience was the worst of its kind, did that not imply that other experiences of its kind were bound to be better?

I was sure it did, but, try as I might, I could not bring to mind a new set of upside-down eyes with which to fall in love. The problem was my tongue. The tip of it had gone to exploring around my mouth. Besides pushing into the hole where my front tooth used to be, which it had been doing constantly for a month, it was taking an interest in other things. For instance, it had found a bump on my gum at the end of the lower left-hand row of molars. It had discovered that, by putting pressure on this bump, it could produce quite considerable pain.

Just then, a little curtain parted in my head and the true future was revealed. I saw myself returning to the tacky office of Dr. Bismark. I was carrying flowers of apology for Ethel, his aged assistant. I was apologizing for my outburst and for the new front tooth, for having acquired it through the services of another practitioner of the dental art.

Dr. Bismark reclined me in his dirty green chair and poked at the bump in my lower gum. His face was upside-down to mine but it didn't bother me. His glasses were so covered in dust and dandruff I could hardly see his eyes at all.

The Hockey Widow

September

SID AND JARVIS, DIGGER AND STEADMAN WERE DOWN IN the basement drafting players for their hockey pool. This meant it was September.

Rita pulled a sheet of homemade pizza from the oven and slid it across the burners. She considered how many trips it was apt to take her to get the pizza, plates and napkins, and four cold beer downstairs.

Her recently deceased mother's voice: *If they want food let them come and get it themselves. What are you, their donkey?*

She imagined going downstairs (why not take the pizza?) and saying this, how they would all either not look at her or, if she bellowed, how they would look up in a lost daze, the way kids look when awakened in the middle of the night.

What about your kids? Pianos tied to their bums?

As if on cue, Lisa entered the room. What she had tied to her body were neon green, street hockey goalie pads. In one hockey-gloved hand, she carried a plastic goalie stick. On the other hand, her baseball mitt. She was heading for the door.

"It's dark out," Rita said automatically. The TV is on.

School starts at nine. It's snowing. She wondered when she would stop saying things like this.

Rita examined her daughter. Hair chopped short, sweatshirt and jeans. No trace of feminine adornment. Lisa would be eleven in a few months and Rita remembered her saying recently with a kind of exasperation, "I guess I'll get breasts soon." She so obviously viewed it as a negative development, an impediment in her struggle to be as good as any boy in the most male of all arenas: the hockey rink.

Rita's thoughts, as usual, had gone on too long. Before she could ever decide what it was she needed to say to her daughter, her daughter was gone. Looking through the darkened living room and out the bay window, she could see the ball hockey game in progress, could faintly hear it between the shouts from the basement.

And she wasn't about to ask Willy to help. He'd be in his room, reading or drawing, or cutting things out of magazines to paste in his scrapbook. She wouldn't do it: make him a victim of his own absurd good will again.

Rita chopped the pizza into large squares then put her oven mitts back on. Please, Mother, not another word. She carried the pizza downstairs.

The air in the rumpus room was blue-grey. Through the gloom, she saw that her husband Sid had rearranged his baseball cap so the visor sat in the middle of his head, pointing up. She wouldn't ask. The card table was covered in newspaper clippings, note pads, ashtrays, beer cans (some of them crushed). It was apparently Sid's turn to pick and the others were grinning at him with hyenalike anticipation.

"This is the pits," he exclaimed. "You've got me cornered."

Rita set the pizza on a metal, floral-patterned TV tray, rolled it up to the table.

"Burns, then! I'll take bloody Burns, the wimp." The others guffawed. Steadman, wearing a cowboy hat, reached up and put a hockey card in the band.

Rita was on the stairs again, headed for the napkins, plates and beer. It angered her that she knew exactly what Sid's words meant. Sid hated the local NHL hockey team, the Bisons, like poison. They were losers. Doug Burns was the team's highest scorer and the vicissitudes of the draft system had just trapped Sid into picking Burns against his staunchly held policy of never drafting Bisons players. The hockey card Steadman put in his hat band was likely one of Burns so that Sid would have to look at it throughout the rest of the evening.

I told you. Don't tell me I didn't tell you. Nip it in the bud, I said.

For crying out loud, Mother, you did say that but I never recall you ever saying how.

Rita was back with the plates and the beer.

"Rosteen."

"Digger, you jerk, he went two rounds ago."

"Ya, get in the game, Dig."

Digger was from Australia. He was expected to screw up like this. But, through a series of what the others called flukes and examples of dumb luck, Digger had won the $600 last year. No more nice guy from the others.

Rita looked at the cluttered table and began clamping together more TV trays. She rolled them into place, set out the plates and napkins, scooped out pieces of pizza, snapped the beer cans and put them on the trays. She reached in for the empties and even dumped the ashtrays. Still, not one of them acknowledged her presence or touched his pizza. Living in the land of the cliché: a hockey widow.

"All right, all right," said Digger. He reached up under his Los Angeles Kings jersey and scratched expressively. "Forbes ain't gone. I'll take Forbes."

"Perfect, Digger. But just so you know, he's got collateral damage in his left knee and probably won't play until Christmas."

"I read it was a third degree strain. In which case he'll be back by December, unless the anthroscopic surgery shows up complications."

"Who's turn is it?"

Rita almost yelled *pizza* but was glad she didn't. If she had to tell her children that it was dark, snowing or Saturday, she refused to do the same for her husband and his dumb friends.

"I hope you all get third degree fractures in the collateral ventricles of your skullbones." She wasn't more than three feet away when she said this, picking up some crumpled balls of notepaper, but there was no pleasure in it. Like screaming you deaf old ninny in the ear of a deaf old ninny.

Back upstairs, Rita tiptoed to her son's closed door, listened guiltily to the silence within. Willy was thirteen. He didn't listen to music on the tape deck she'd got him in hopes that he would. To please her, he had used it once to record the audio off *The Nature of Things*. She wished she wasn't hoping that the silence meant he was masturbating.

"Willy? Are you busy?"

"Not really, Mom. Come on in."

She pushed open the door. Willy was spraddled on his bed, cosy against a backrest of bunched pillows. He was reading a library book, one that seemed too thick and dun-coloured for a boy so young and thin.

"What are you reading, Will?"

"Aw, just some more about the ozone layer thing. You know, global warming." The smile on Will's face, so dependable, had the recent worry shining through.

Rita thought of the line that would follow if this were a TV sit-com. *What's that got to do with you?* She felt as if she had said it. In one way or another, she was always pushing her son toward things that seemed more suitable to the interests of a boy his age – except hockey; she had not and would not push him there.

"It's pretty bad, Mom. I'm not sure the world's going to get it together in time."

"It might though, Will. When I was a girl, people didn't even know about the dangers and now I think most everyone does."

"But it says here...."

"Will!"

She hated her tone, stopped herself. It was the tone in which the TV mom would ask what that had to do with him.

"It's okay, Mom," said her Will, smiling dependably. "We don't need to talk about it all the time. What are the others doing?"

"Dad and his crew are still at it downstairs. Lisa's out playing street hockey."

They shared the moment then, the one that Rita had to admit was the best these days had to offer: she and her son sitting on his bed with weary, knowledgeable smiles on. Smiles that said what? What did they say? Here we are, trapped in the hockey nut house. Or: kids will be kids.

"Don't stay up reading too late, Will. You don't want to wake up with a headache."

"Sure, Mom. Thanks." And boom. He was back into the disaster-filled pages: watching the plumes of combusted fossil fuels rising into the damaged sky.

January

On an ice cold day, Rita was downtown, shopping from an endless list. A chequebook register in her head had been subtracting steadily from a not very big balance.

The cold half of the year had turned into a time of financial disaster for her family. Back-to-school items and Sid's fall hockey pools were just the beginning. Then came the six-month bill for his welding truck insurance, new hockey equipment for Lisa if she'd grown, some new pieces of hockey gear for Sid usually, too. Then Christmas. Pretty soon it would be Lisa's birthday, then Sid's, then Will's.

But the huge one, the cost that Rita couldn't believe Sid saddled them with annually, was his season ticket to watch the Bisons, a team he hated. When she complained about the season ticket, Sid would fly into a diatribe as predictable in timing and direction as any migration of birds. He worked hard, he would say; he had few amusements; he was awfully lucky to have the season ticket and, if he gave it up, would probably never get another one.

Five years ago when the Bisons came to their city, Rita had been caught up in Sid's childish delight over it all. She had agreed about the season ticket, had even felt a measure of anxiety when he took his sleeping bag down to sleep outside the Bisons ticket office. What if they ran out just as his turn came? She had accepted it all so easily because, back then, Sid did work hard as a welder and was paying off his welding truck at record speed. At that time, it was also true that he had few amusements.

Well, things had changed. They had changed so completely

it was impossible to believe Sid had failed to notice. *Few amusements?* Relative to whom, Rita wondered. Prince Andrew? His hockey drafts, his "fat man" hockey team, his going out to watch Bisons home games and all the other games he watched with his buddies on the big screen down at the bar. Then there was his hockey card collection and his careful supervision of Lisa's.

Sid played constantly, as far as Rita could see, but she also realized that, somewhere along the line, Sid had ceased to view any of it as play. The season's ticket and the hockey cards were *investments*. The hockey pools were *business*. The fat man recreational hockey league (in spite of the gallons of beer and all the cigarettes afterward) was *exercise*. And the proof that none of it was play was that *none of it was fun*.

In the morning when he read the newspaper before leaving for work, Sid would curse and swear, really angry, over the latest Bisons's loss or his having slipped down in any of his hockey pools. He and all the other guys on the fat man hockey team took it so seriously that they booked ice in the middle of the night to practice. During the games, they fought.

Rita stopped herself. It took some exertion. *Look at yourself,* her mother was saying and she did.

She was standing in a hockey card store. She had been standing over one of the glass cases for a long time, who knows what crazy expression on her face. It was even possible that she'd talked some of her thoughts out loud. A young kid in a baseball cap was on the opposite side of the glass case, looking bemused and superior.

"Something I can help you with, ma'am?" he asked.

"I'll let you know," Rita snapped.

The kid drifted off to a boy Will's age and they argued over whether you could spot a rare premium card by its colour through the edge of the plastic wrapper in Super Pro Series I. Rita had heard Lisa and Sid debate the same point at home and wondered when these two would get around to the related topic of weighing the wax packs of another set to detect which ones contained the holograms.

Rita tried to decipher Sid's writing on a piece of soiled notepaper: directions on what cards to buy Lisa for her birthday. Some Russian player's rookie card, "but make sure it's centred." Any Guy Lafleur cards from the mid-seventies. There was a list of prices for these that she wasn't permitted to go above. "Mint!" God help her if she failed to notice a wax deposit or a nubbed corner.

Rita had stood here for so long she was getting embarrassed. She kept losing focus on the cards in the case, seeing instead the fray on the cuff of her winter coat. And now there was a man standing beside her at the same case, a fact that exerted another kind of pressure on her to leave. But she had to get the cards, either that or come all the way down here again before Lisa's birthday.

Having looked so long at her own cuff and sleeve, she couldn't help but notice the sleeve on the man's coat. He had on a fine dark blue overcoat, good wool and brand new. His hand lying on the case close to hers, fingers gently drumming, was hard to figure. It looked like a rich person's hands, the nails so clean and carefully clipped, but there were also little nicks and bruises on it. When she was pretty sure he was looking elsewhere, at the kid who ran the store, she chanced a look up at the man's face.

It was a nice face, clean-shaven, a well-defined angle of jaw. Then she saw that it was also a familiar face, very familiar, and when it came to her that it was the face of Doug Burns, the Bisons centre, it came with such a rush that she said the name aloud.

"Doug Burns."

The next few seconds were bad. He swung round to her. He looked startled, even frightened, she thought.

"Yes?" he said, and he said it so timidly, as if he were a child caught fooling around behind teacher's back. Rita tried to think why. They were in a hockey card shop, he was a hockey player; maybe there was something odd, embarrassing, about his being in such a place.

"Oh," Rita said. "I just recognized you and your name popped out." It was the truth.

He smiled at her – risked a smile you might say. His face

really was very pleasant. There were hardly any marks on it and his smile was full of wonderfully white teeth. Rita was encouraged by the smile and, with a sort of what-the-heck feeling, she asked, "But what would you be doing here? Do you collect cards?"

She had not intended for him to become as badly rattled as he now became. "No, I, I, just sort of, came in." He was so obviously lying that she was desperate to stop him, to protect him. "Oh, never mind," she said. "It's not important."

Perhaps grateful to her, he didn't ask the same question back. But he seemed to want to say something. He looked around, his feet might have been glued down. The kids in the store, the one running it too, they were all watching them now. Burns seemed afraid of them.

Rita took control. She called over the bemused, superior kid and she asked him, "Do you have a Doug Burns card, his rookie?"

"Ya, I do. It's here."

"Is it mint?"

"I'd say so, ya."

It was four dollars.

"A bargain," said Rita and bought it.

Then she turned to Doug Burns and she said, "Would you join me for a cup of coffee?"

"Ya, sure," he said and they left together with the group in the store circling round into a scrum to discuss who that was and what they might have done in the way of an autograph if the bimbo lady hadn't beaten them to the rookie card. Then again *Beckett's* only listed Burns's rookie at two bucks, mint. Even signed it probably wasn't worth the four she paid.

The part of town they were in was a former slum. It had been rescued from the wrecking ball about the time the city got its NHL franchise. The upper floors of the reclaimed brick buildings were spartan still and rented cheap: perfect for marginal businesses like card collector shops. The main floors were fancier: import boutiques, book stores, vegetarian restaurants and gourmet coffee bars. Into one of the latter, Rita bravely led Doug Burns.

She felt strangely courageous and, in her head, the worn knee-length winter coat was transforming into something smart and furry. Her battered car full of groceries at the soon-to-be-expired meter had become the possession and problem of someone else, someone with a less attractive coat and manner. In fact, Rita felt the way she had before she met Sid, when she had been in university for social work and the future had always seemed fuzzy but bright, like a sunrise in a snowstorm.

She went straight to the counter and, turning to Doug Burns, asked, "Cappuccino?" He nodded. She took a table right next to the curved window, facing right onto the street. She was determined not to lose momentum. Everything she had ever heard about Burns was sharp and ready in her mind, every belittling thing Sid and Lisa had ever said about him, and there'd been plenty.

"My name is Rita," she said, extending her hand through the frayed sleeve. His hand was cool and rough, without any macho grip in it, she noted. Everyone Sid had ever introduced her to, man, woman and child, had tried promptly to break her hand. Burns mumbled something about it being nice to meet her too. He really was very shy.

"Do you like hockey, Doug?" This was a crazy question, impertinent too, but there was considerable doubt in her household that he did.

"Oh, I don't know," he said. The question was certainly a tough one for him. "It's a good job, I try to look at it like that. I don't know what else I would do."

"You don't like hockey as much as most players, then."

He winced but then seemed to gather some courage of his own. He asked, "What about you, Rita? Do you like hockey?"

"I hate it with all my soul."

Burns laughed, suddenly and loud, like he'd been jabbed with an electrical prong right in the little zone of his brain labelled "Laugh Centre." His laugh had the same effect on Rita: zing to the laugh centre and the only trouble was what they were going to do when the laughing stopped. Things did become silent but Burns was every bit as determined as Rita to get over this obstacle and go on.

"Why would you be in a sports card store then?" he asked.

Rita's mother started up, something about being absolutely frank about who you are, about your status. Status in her mother's terms meant nothing for a woman but marital status. Shut up, Mother.

"A birthday present for a child I know. You know how it is, it's a hockey-mad city." Rita enjoyed the fact that, technically, no word she said was a lie. "And you, Doug?"

"Same thing. A kid I'm related to wanted my rookie card and I didn't have one."

"Oh, oh," said Rita, partly in recognition of her having snaffled the card he wanted, partly registering concern that the kid he was related to might be related to him as Lisa was to her. She raced through her mental file on Burns – unmarried, she was almost certain. And that brought up the fact of his being probably a decade younger than her. She cut off both thoughts with the appropriate apology for taking the card he came to the shop to buy. But she didn't offer to give it to him.

"Oh, not to worry," he said. "There must be others around. I guess I hope there are. I'm not that hot an item."

"No? You're always the top scorer, aren't you?"

"On one of the worst teams in history. But how do you know that if you don't like hockey?"

Another challenge. Another order to her mother to keep silent. "It's like if there was a war on," Rita said, amazed at how easy this was. "The news is all around you all the time. You can't help but know things."

"Ya, I see what you mean." He was shy again and then: "Did you want the card autographed? Kids usually like that. It ups the value a bit."

"Of course." She produced the card and she noticed for the first time how very young Doug was in the picture. It was an action shot, the fake kind with the helmet off. He had longer hair and a sort of frightened look on his post-adolescent face. He signed it with a special kind of autographing pen that lets you see the picture through the writing.

"Nice signature," she said. The writing had large loops and the "B" in Burns looked like it had breasts. Oh, dear.

"Do you ever think about things like global warming?" she asked. Another insane question but the instinct was a good one. He brightened right away.

"I sure do. I don't know why but I think about those kinds of disasters all the time, more than I should. Why?"

"I do too, that's all."

Rita felt a pressure building, a pressure to leave and a sense that she shouldn't fight this one. It was timing. To stay too long would be to invite some kind of complication she couldn't weave her way around. She took a last drink of her coffee and pushed the cup an inch ahead. She was certain that, with this man, this Doug Burns, the action would be read precisely as meant.

"I guess you have to go," he said, with just the right amount of regret.

"Yes, I do but I wanted to ask, how is it that you have such nice teeth?"

This caused another strange flurry in Burns. His hand started toward his mouth. Then it stopped and pulled back to the table by some opposite force.

"They really look okay?"

"Really. They're great teeth."

"One of the front ones is fake."

"I'd never have known."

"It's new. I lost a tooth in Montreal awhile back and had to get this false one." He pointed up at his mouth. She couldn't tell which tooth he was pointing at. She told him that and he rewarded her with an enormous smile that did, frankly, reveal a little something, a wire maybe, over the top of his left front tooth. She tried desperately not to even think this in words, so perceptive was the communication between them.

"I really want to thank you for the coffee and the talk," he was saying. "It gets pretty lonely sometimes when all people want to talk about is hockey."

"I know what you mean. It's great to find someone who actually plays professional hockey and still knows it isn't the whole world."

"It sure isn't."

A lull into which both of them wanted to leap. At the same time it mattered a great deal who did the leaping and how. It was for him to do. A sort of silent consensus had to be achieved before they could move on.

"Do you think it would be possible for us to have dinner sometime?"

"Yes, it would be possible," she said. "How about the sixth of February?"

Burns popped a little hinged card out of his inside jacket pocket and looked inside it. "That would be great. Well, maybe not. We're in town that night but we've got a game. It would have to be a pretty late dinner."

"Perfect. I like to eat late. Have you got a number? So we can figure out where and so on closer to the date?"

He gave her another card from the same pocket, a simple one with just his name and phone number. Having put that in her purse, Rita got up quickly and was suddenly outside and walking fast.

All the way back to the car she had to put up with her mother. Once she had the ticket picked off the windshield and was in the car, she put a stop to it. *You always said I should do something about it, didn't you, Mother? Well now I am.*

February

"Care for another glass of wine, Doug?"

Doug Burns had just finished a giant plate of lasagna (his favourite, he said) and he dabbed neatly at his mouth with the cloth napkin before saying that, yes, he thought he could have another glass. Rita reached with the bottle and poured until he held his hand out flat. He was being very careful about how much he drank.

Rita fingered the pearl necklace she had put on for the occasion and watched him take a tiny sip. What a really delicious man he was. It was a shame what she had done to him but, really, what other way was there?

"How about you, Sid?"

Sid had taken Lisa to the Boston game. This being her

birthday, he'd talked Steadman into giving her his ticket. Sitting on the same side of the table, they were both quiet and still confused. "I'll stick to beer," he said grumpily.

"Will, would you help me for a moment in the kitchen?" She looked at her son and mouthed the word cake. While they walked out toward the kitchen, there was silence behind them. But before the kitchen door swung shut, Rita heard Doug ask Lisa what she thought of the game.

Will hadn't been in on the secret either and he was beside himself, as childishly delighted as Rita could remember him being. While plunking wax candles into the chocolate icing, he whispered, "How did you do it, Mom? How did you *meet* him?"

"Just bumped into him one day and we went for coffee." She was retaining her mystery.

"It's great. I thought Dad was going to blow a vessel when he came to the door."

It had been quite a moment. Sid and Lisa had only been back from the game fifteen minutes. Rita had told them there would be a mystery guest, coming late for dinner and cake. "What the hell have you done now?" Sid had asked. He was in a slightly blacker mood than usual because the Bisons had not only lost but had been shut out. He specifically complained about Doug Burns. "He's the guy supposed to score for that crowd."

Then the doorbell and Doug Burns was there in person, already looking a bit troubled. He was wearing a suit and bearing gifts: flowers and a bottle of wine. The only really sad part came next, when she'd had to step outside, to whisper close to his ear, "I'm sorry, Doug."

She hadn't underestimated him, though. After only a few seconds of looking hurt, Doug rallied. Rita led him in, introduced him to her open-mouthed husband and daughter, to her broadly grinning son, and he'd been very polite, as if the scene was exactly what he expected. The flowers were a problem. He was holding them low and slightly behind him. Rita leaned down and took them from him. "Doug, you really are sweet." She swung around and placed the bundle in Lisa's arms. "Mr. Burns brought you roses for your birthday, dear. Wasn't that nice?"

Now Rita carried the flaming cake into the dining room

with Will walking ahead carrying the presents and starting the song. Doug sang with gusto, Rita noted. Lisa blew out the candles, Rita cut the cake, Lisa opened her gifts. She opened the little flat one first: Doug Burns's signed rookie card.

It was in that moment that Lisa departed the camp of her father, and, perhaps, though it was too soon to say, from the camp of all those who give their lives to hockey. Almost tearful, she said, "Ahhh," the note rising sharply at the end. "Is that ever neat?" And she got up and walked to Doug Burns, and gave him a hug.

Her final doubts extinguished now like the birthday candles, Rita passed the plates of cake around, serving Doug first. Then she sat back and watched and listened for the short time that Doug could stay. Touching her flowers and the rookie card, ignoring both her parents, Lisa asked Doug a few things about hockey players that she'd always wanted to know. For instance, did hockey players really high-stick each other so often deliberately, or was it just their sticks getting bumped up high by accident? Doug said that, whichever it was, he wished he could afford to wear a spherical helmet of clear indestructable plastic like an astronaut. Lisa laughed.

Will managed to get the topic around for a while to the atmospheric effects of aerosol cans. Doug said that he didn't understand the connection between aerosol and ozone but he was always careful to use the stick kind of deodorant all the same. Given the amount of deodorant a hockey player goes through, he reckoned his contribution was significant. Everyone laughed, even Sid.

At one point, Doug asked the mostly silent Sid if he had any interest in hockey; he was certainly giving the impression tonight that he might not have. Sid, for the first time in memory, did not know quite what to say on a hockey topic. "Oh, you know," he said, finally, "I guess I have an average interest."

It was about then that Rita paused to address her mother. *See*, she said. *It worked, didn't it?* What's more, Rita suspected it was going to keep on working for awhile. Not that this night would ever be replicated. She was realistic enough to know that

Doug and she were very unlikely to meet again. But the effects, they might go on.

While Will and Lisa tried to talk to Doug at the same time, while he took the politest look at his watch, while Sid sat looking down at his uneaten chocolate cake (his favourite, in fact), Rita took the opportunity to have a long last look at Doug Burns. There was more than a little halo of regret around her heart as she did. To be a mother and a wife is to sacrifice for your family. That was one of her mother's nuggets. *To a point.* That was another.

When she stopped looking at Doug, Rita noticed that Sid's attention had moved from his cake over to her. She looked Sid right in the eye, right where the little worry was centred, and she repeated that thought very loudly. *To a point!*

Positive Images

1

*I*LOST MY FIRST TOOTH TO HOCKEY IN THE MIDDLE OF my fourth NHL season and, being the kind of fierce competitor that I am, I said: that's it, I quit. I was fond of and proud of my teeth. I counted on them to assist me in some lucrative hockey afterlife. Most of all, I counted on them to help me attract a woman before I left hockey and lost the only edge I have. But there it was: at the end of a lopsided game in Montreal, in the time it takes to lose a draw, a twenty-two-year-old maniac had driven his helmet into my mouth and disfigured me for life.

That same night, I phoned my agent, Bernie. Through a mouthful of blood-soaked cotton batting, I told him of my decision to leave hockey. I thought I was ready for anything he might throw at me but the bastard tricked me. He cried.

For some unaccountable reason, perhaps that I was in mourning over the recent death in my mouth and near tears myself, Bernie's crying touched me deeply – much more, for example, than when he said, "After all that I've done for you,

Burns." I honestly couldn't think what that might be. Taking a greedy cut of my salary didn't seem particularly heroic. Then I decided he must mean the only endorsement contract he'd ever negotiated on my behalf: a TV spot for Uniglobe, a manufacturer of athletic supporters and cans.

The first image in the commercial was a defenceman wearing a Lone Ranger mask, winding up in slow motion for a slap shot. At the top of his wind-up, real motion kicks in and he smashes the puck toward the camera. The screen goes black. The sound of broken glass. Cut to me in a suit, standing in front of an empty net, holding the contraption on the palm of my hand. "Uniglobe," I say. "Believe me, it makes a difference."

Besides a modest amount of quickly spent cash, this television appearance gained me a nickname. That's right: "Glass Balls." Worse still, part of my contract was that I had to wear a Uniglobe for the whole season. It had a lot of snaps and straps and, when it was on, it looked like a lady's garter belt. In the heat of play, the snaps came unfastened and, back on the bench, I spent most of my time working it back up my hockey sock. This caused trouble with the TV station that broadcast our home games. "Every time we cut to your bench," they said, "Burns is playing with himself."

But the night of the loss of my tooth, Bernie's tears over the telephone sawed through my resolve and on down through all the things I held against him. These whimpers and snorts made a lot more sense two years later when Bernie was busted at the Toronto airport for a large bag of white stuff taped into his armpit. After his conviction, he revealed all in hopes of getting a book out of it. Referring back to the time of our telephone conversation, he claimed his habit was topping two thousand dollars a week.

I knew nothing of this at the time. I just thought Bernie had bad sinuses and a rare case of moustache dandruff and, in this precise moment, was all torn up to think that our business friendship was over. Feeling myself slipping, I trotted out the line I'd been rehearsing all evening.

"A missing tooth is a hole in your head for life, Bernie."

There was a loud double snort on the line. "And a million out of your wallet is a hole in your head since birth."

I bit. "What million?"

"The million I can get you over two seasons."

"Hold on. You mean four." My current salary was $270,000. While it was true the team was keen to renegotiate my contract, an upward direction in the salary figure wasn't what they had in mind.

"No!" More coughs and splutters. Poor guy, I thought. Broken heart. "Two. Three tops."

"What do you know, Bernie?"

"I've had my ear to the ice, okay?" More like his nose in the snow. "Trust me."

Trust an agent. Weird notion.

"There's no way, Bernie. Mr. Topworth can't afford it."

"Who says Topworth will own the team next year? Who says the team will even be in the same city? That's all I'm saying, Burns. Don't be a fool."

So was I a fool? Did I quit hockey the night of the violent appearance of a gap in my smile? No, I did not. But the reasons had nothing to do with Bernie or with money, and very little to do with hockey. The simple truth was that, as I lay in bed that night, a mouth full of pain and unable to sleep, I was set upon by visions of myself in the life I would lead outside of hockey. I saw myself in a predictable assortment of menial jobs and I saw myself always alone, alone and wishing I had stayed in hockey long enough to find a wife.

Whatever my opinion of hockey as a sport, I have always respected it as a means of getting homely, dull-witted men superior wives. The undeniable proof had come the previous summer when I was called upon to stand at the side of my cornerman Smitty Smith, and to hand him a ring which he tried to jam onto the wrong finger of a young woman named Pearl. Now, it's not up to me to say what Pearl wasn't; but she was the reasonably attractive hostess of a rib joint where Smitty regularly reduced the equivalent of a yearling steer to a pile of bones on his plate. She did manage to read a romance novel every two weeks. And once, when Smitty miscounted his bill by twenty or so dollars, she did pursue him into the parking lot and demand restitution.

And there she was, suddenly united in matrimony to a man who, when signing the register after his vows, looked like he was trying to part the facets of a diamond with a pickaxe.

Smitty, married. And yet, there I stood beside him, rather dapper in my tuxedo, almost handsome and unmarked as hockey players go – and single. Woefully single.

In all those seasons of nights of sitting in bars replacing fluids after games, when women would gather and pairings were made, I could never seem to strike the right balance. Burke, our captain, noticing how I always turned women away or was turned away by them, offered this advice: "You always think you're too good, Burns, except when you think you're not good enough." This, from no Rhodes Scholar, was true.

Eight times out of ten, a woman leaning my way would do something or say something that put me totally off. It could be so small: reaching down and making a sound of fingernail on nylon that I couldn't bear; or saying that I reminded her of a movie star and, pressed for details, naming some jerk I disliked; or just a mention of some other hockey player she had "known." Virginity isn't a big issue with me but the idea of another hockey player, some empty-mouthed, scarred behemoth ... it didn't bear thinking about then and it doesn't now.

I said eight out of ten times were like that. Number nine was the result of my standing around expensive hotel lobbies striking what I thought were intriguing, man-of-the-world poses. This worked for James Bond and it worked for me too. Often a woman would appear by my side, asking for a light or some such conversation starter. In my best James Bond style, I would compliment her loveliness and suggest a drink after the game (thus working in that I was a professional hockey player). And every damn time this happened, later, in the intimacy of her room, she would turn out to be a call girl.

No matter how much I spent on clothes and hair stylists, no matter how hard I practised my poses in front of the bathroom mirror, there was just no fooling these ladies. They could spot a fat wallet on a farm boy's hip through any get-up, at any distance. Alas, I was not nearly as good at spotting them and, time after time, I'd wind up in a hotel room shelling out her atrociously high fee for nothing.

Now if that sounds like a lie, consider how hard I have worked in the heat of the hockey wars to keep my good health and looks. No condom in the world is thick enough to console my fear of sexually transmitted, incurable disease. And because I always felt it was my fault, not theirs, I always paid. If their professional ethics demanded that they do something for me in return, I'd request a backrub and "no funny stuff." During this backrub, I would often tell about my pining search for a wife, my desperate belief that pro hockey would help me find one. It owed me that much at least.

The tenth time was the woman I admired. A woman who did nothing to repel me and much to attract me; who, to my knowledge, had never met a hockey player before; who was as frightened of sex with strangers as I was. As Burke put it: the woman for whom I felt not good enough. When such a rare woman came within range of my wooing, I would do one of two things: I would slink away in a fit of sulking self-pity, or I would fawn (which, defined by the Oxford Dictionary, means "trying to win attention or affection by crouching close and trying to lick"). And, while fawning, I would make a funny sound scratching a bruise through my trouser leg, or I would tell her she looked like a movie star and, when pressed, would name the wrong one. If she didn't feel she was too good for me at the outset, I wouldn't let up on her until she did.

All this came to me in the sleepless night after the loss of my tooth and, by dawn, I had decided I couldn't quit hockey, not yet. I would wait until the end of the season and, given that the Bisons were once again virtually out of the playoffs by midseason, that meant I had exactly thirty-eight games to change my luck and find a woman to admire who could admire me back.

When thirty-eight games had dwindled down to twenty, my dignity crumbled. I phoned Helmet Soffshel, who was listed in the Yellow Pages as a professional publicist. I told him I wanted to throw a party for myself in the penthouse suite of the city's grandest hotel.

"But what's the occasion?" Helmet kept asking. "There must be an occasion."

"It's the occasion of my desperately needing a wife," I told him.

"Ooh, pathetic," he said. "That won't do at all."

On this point I agreed with Helmet and it was to give the party a respectable purpose that I publicly admitted my plan to retire. The party became my preretirement bash, my paean of praise to the game of my life.

Everything had to be paid for in advance: caviar, canapes, champagne, a tasteful, three-piece jazz ensemble, napkins and matchbooks with my name and career-span specially printed on, a battalion of black-tie waiters, a good-looking hostess. To be honest, when I got a load of Renata, the hostess, a striking Cleopatra with hair like spun coal, I almost asked her to marry me on the spot. If she had happened by some miracle to say yes, I could have reached my goal at a fraction of the cost. Between Renata and Helmet, my bank account had begun to make a noise like an aircraft toilet flushing.

"But will there be women?" I nagged Helmet whenever he served me with a fresh passel of bills. He didn't strike me as having a lot of experience in that regard.

"I'm working on it," he'd say and I never cared for the struggle this implied.

Helmet insisted that I must not be visible for the first half hour of my party. I stayed in the back bedroom in a ridiculously overgroomed state, standing arms out like a scarecrow so as not to tax my deodorant. I also looked in all the drawers for a Bible but apparently Gideons don't do penthouse suites. One of my odd habits in those days was to read the last book of the Bible whenever I was in a hotel room. The part about the end of the world spoke to me personally.

Without biblical assistance that night, I had to content

myself with apocalyptic daydreams. Four horses on skates breathed fire and other kinds of warming corruption on the world until they had it completely melted, including both polar ice caps. All of creation drowned except for a handful of goats and a few Sherpas, the latter setting out immediately to build an ark of *krumholz*. What they should have been building were skates. After the apocalypse, the world cooled off rapidly. It cooled, it froze; it became a uniform sphere of gleaming ice.

"Okay, Dougie, let's go."

Helmet stood in the bedroom doorway, in a crimson tuxedo and royal purple cummerbund. He beckoned me into the party room. Confetti and streamers flew; the band kicked into a tasteful rendition of "For He's a Jolly Good Fellow." Just before I was blinded by flashbulbs, which presumably I was also paying for, I saw enough to sink my hopes titanically. In the blue and orange blindness that followed, an item in one of Helmet's recent ledgers pulsed in neon: "Guests – $2,000." When my vision cleared, I went around the room greeting my teammates, their superior wives, a few reporters – and a reunion of local and regional call girls, many of whom had given me expert and expensive backrubs.

In its way it was a nice party and, at times, dancing with the call girls or the superior wives, I felt little surges of sentimentality for the game I was leaving. When Smitty felt compelled to dump the ice and fruit from an empty punch bowl over my head, I laughed. A few minutes later I undid his bright red suspenders at the back and pulled down his trousers to reveal his boxer shorts with the cartoons, front and back. It was fun but, at the end of the night, when the guests paraded past me at the door, my mood was plunging past all previously known lower horizons.

When the last guest had gone, I turned and faced the dismantling of my dreams for the evening. Helmet was marshalling the serving crew for a cleanup of empty glasses and plates; the band members were storing their equipment away into black cases; and Renata, the hostess, was approaching me with a slip of paper in her hand; Renata, beautiful, stoic, emotionally featureless, to whom the clockwork efficiency of the party owed so much.

Seeing the slip of paper, I reached automatically for my wallet.

"A success?" she asked crisply.

"No," I answered, too depressed to worry about its being an insult to her craft.

"You didn't find a woman."

I wanted at that moment to pull off Helmet's cummerbund with such force that he spun a hole through all twenty-nine floors of the building.

"Of course I knew," she said. "I had to."

"I didn't meet anyone."

"Yes, you did."

And she poked the slip of paper into my jacket pocket, right on top of my red silk puff handkerchief.

2

Yes, the note on top of my puff handkerchief contained Renata's full name, address and phone number. It was significant that the data was handwritten on paper rather than machine-printed on a business card. That very evening, Renata had decided to marry me, subject to a review of my assets.

Because I was busy with a writing project and Renata was enrolled in one of those deep immersion "How To Make A Million" courses, our wedding didn't take place until two months after the end of the season. Smitty had a particularly long and snorty laughing fit during the ceremony and the severe lady Justice of the Peace had to interrupt her recitation twice while the old cornerman got hold of himself.

I can't really remember anything else – except for one thing. I remember the part of the wedding involving the ring. First, Smitty had some trouble getting the ring box out of his trouser pocket. He tickled himself to more laughter in the process. I opened the blue box myself because he didn't realize he was supposed to. Taking the wedding band, I swivelled to where Renata's finger was waiting. At that precise instant, I hesitated, not because I was having second thoughts but because the engagement ring already there on her finger looked unfamiliar. I could not recognize it at all. I'd been there for the purchase, a peripheral figure with a chequebook while Renata and the salesperson talked carats and facets, and I did have a good look at the ring while shelling out the megabucks. But I swear the one she wore at our wedding looked different. I didn't mention this, of course, and I slipped the wedding band on beside it dainty as can be. Then I snapped Renata a worried look. I was afraid I would see a stranger's face inside the veil.

We honeymooned in Vegas and had our first argument when Renata wanted to see Wayne Newton and I wanted to see an illusionist who claimed he could cut an elephant into thirds. Renata couldn't wait to get home. When we did return, she transformed into something you'd need high technology equipment to photograph. My eyes weren't up to the test and what I remember of the ensuing months is a series of blurs: a blurred figure rolling on blurred stockings and applying blurred make-up in front of the bedroom mirror of a house so new and strange it scared me every morning; blurred lips at the telephone while I waited on my side of the bed pretending to read *Esquire*.

To use the management phrase, Renata put my money to work. Me too. Besides buying as much real estate as my money could mortgage, she attached my still-recognizable name to every worthy cause in the city. When she left the bedroom and the house each day, and my head cleared of the blur of her, I would find a list on the bedside table. I never saw her make this list but it was always there. Place, time, contact person, cause, suggested dress and, in quotation marks, a sentence she wanted me to say. "A progressive zoo is one of the most valuable institutions a city can have." "Integration of the handicapped into the mainstream of society is one of the most important challenges facing us today." I lived in fear of mixing them up.

The closest I ever came to seeing Renata still in those days was a moment in our kitchen in the eighth month of marriage. I came out in my bathrobe to find her, amazingly, still there at 9:00 AM. The still moment was the pause before she said, "Doug, you're no longer bankable." It is important to record that she said this without accusation or pity; more in the way you might say, "The milk company no longer delivers." She went on to say that she was staging me out of the worthy cause business and that I had a choice: I could have an office and a meaningless job in her growing empire, or I could do nothing. I told her I thought nothing was more my line.

Nothing. How extraordinarily difficult it is to do. In my opinion, doing nothing is a worthy cause and one of the greatest challenges facing our society today. I don't think anyone does it very well.

So I failed at doing nothing and, after I failed, I had a breakdown. At least that's what Renata said I had. What happened was that I went stealthily about finding out what assets and savings plans were still in my name. For some mysterious tax reason, several things were. The house I had never thought of as anything but Renata's house turned out to be mine.

I went to a bank with paper evidence of my collateral and I told them I wanted to start a chain of doughnut shops. When asked what experience I had, I told them I was an ex-professional hockey player just like the late Tim Horton. The bank's loans manager was very uppity but, when enough earthly chattels had been piled opposite the transaction, the loan was approved.

Many would not view what came next as a success but I do. After months of secret preparations, I opened the three flagships of what I dreamt would soon become a national navy of doughnut outlets. I insisted that the "Opening Soon" banners be dropped at a carefully synchronized instant. Suddenly, there it was, my secret, my pride, revealed to the world.

DOUGIE BURNS DOUGHNUTS

The equipment was primed. Miles of doughnut dough hit the boiling fat. They were good tasting little devils, too. It wasn't until far too late that it occurred to me that *Burns* is a word that should never appear side-by-side with *doughnut*.

People can say what they like about Renata but I think she

behaved very decently that day and right through to the end. In the evening of that quiet opening day, Renata came into my best location, the downtown one, looking splendid in a black suit and blue satin blouse. I remember being grateful that she had left her briefcase in the car. She sat opposite me across a crumb-strewn, doughnut-coloured formica table. I don't think you can surprise Renata and she did not look surprised that night. She looked efficient, like a surgical nurse, and she efficiently told me that no one was going to eat a potentially charred foodstuff, that I had had a breakdown, and that she would stand by me through my period of recovery. She had already booked me into a "resort" in Oregon that specialized in whatever I had.

Despite being there for several months, I don't feel like an authority on the resort that became my next home. If I'm pinned down, I say that broken lives were mended there through the medium of golf. Like most hockey players, I was a better than average golfer already but Skip, my pro at the resort, took several strokes off my score by correctly analyzing the mechanics of my slice and through what he called "positive imaging."

"If you can see yourself hit the ball straight, Dougie, you can hit the ball straight."

Skip said this once a hole and we must have played five thousand holes.

Renata visited every month, on the same day each month, and I looked forward to seeing her even though the visits were pretexts to have me sign things. Early on, I signed papers pertaining to my personal bankruptcy and, later, the papers had to do with our divorce. On her last visit before I was released, she came with two lawyers, one for each of us, and mine took me outside near the first tee and read me the separation agreement. I almost wept at its contents. Renata was leaving me my favourite car and an amount of cash roughly equal to the investment funds she had gained by marrying me. What integrity. What a woman.

I hope people won't think this is a depressing story. I can only relate how I felt the day I left the resort in Oregon. Skip was there with my bags and clubs, helping me get them into my sports car, and he was joking about golf and positive imaging up a storm. I was not feeling as positive as I might have right then because I badly needed a drink. Most folks at the resort were alcoholics and, though never much of a drinker myself, I'd become fond of the adolescent ritual of sneaking out into the bushes each night to drink from their hidden bottles. By the time I was leaving, I had the pencilled outlines of my first and only addiction to alcohol.

The bags and clubs were in the car; the top was up against a light drizzle. Skip was grinning and proclaiming it a beautiful day. I believe he was glad it was raining because that made finding beauty in it a harder positive image to attain. I was shaking his hand, licking dry lips and wondering what in hell I was going to do now. I will never know if this was part of the intended process of my recovery or not but, at that exact instant, a hugely positive good feeling powered through me and burst, drenching me in a shower of itself.

Then I was driving away, down the tree-lined dripping drive. Skip was waving with both hands, a shrinking photograph in my rearview. And I was surging and glowing with all this positive happiness. I'm only twenty-seven, I kept telling myself. Already in this life I have been an NHL hockey player; I've been married to a beautiful woman; I've been an entrepreneur. I've had a bankruptcy, a divorce and a breakdown. I've lost a tooth in a hockey punchup and had it replaced with one almost as good. I'm really living, I told myself, and I knew it was true.

At the stop sign before the Interstate, I confidently signalled left. I drove to the Canadian border. Brimming with positive happiness, I drove home.

Burns Burns Burns and Burns

Two weeks after losing his first tooth to the game of hockey, Doug Burns realized that this was the worst thing that had ever happened to him. He was far from happy with his life but still, losing a tooth, his left front tooth, was the worst. It also came to him that he must correct this disfigurement and get on with the extensive menu of his other problems. Thus Burns entered the offices of Dr. Dent; thus he was introduced to the sultan's tent atmosphere of this supposed place of pain.

I wrote those words and there was a strange pleasure in writing about myself with such telescopic detachment. At the time I wrote it, I was wishing I could live my whole life at that distance. I was playing the remaining games of what I thought would be the last season of my professional hockey career, devilled by a new-found fear that the loss of my first tooth was the beginning of some horrid trend; that, in any game or practice, I could get nailed again, be gashed for stitches, lose an eye, spit out yet more of my teeth.

What the words were supposed to be was the opening of one of the chapters in my book of memoirs. I was on the verge of retirement from hockey, which is to say I was on the verge of possibly endless unemployment, and I had decided to face down that prospect by writing a book about myself. So many hockey nobodies had done this that I thought, why not, why not me too?

Not knowing how you went about this, I called up a few publishers down East. Every one of them asked me who was writing the book. When I said I was, a process began the purpose of which was to get me off the phone as politely but as quickly as possible. When they found out that I was writing my own book, they all suddenly remembered a terrific glut in the hockey life story market.

At this point, I gave birth to a writer. His name was D.P. Burns and old D.P. quickly got on with a campaign of written queries.

Having learned that hockey personality Dougie Burns of the NHL's Bisons franchise is planning to retire at the end of this season, I have become interested in the prospect of writing his memoirs. I have spoken with Burns and he is agreeable. We have begun taping sessions....

By the time D.P. received the replies to his queries, he was well into the book, had written several chapters. But D.P.'s enthusiasm for the project, increased by the process of writing, was not shared by anyone. All of the publishers had found reasons for saying no and, what's more, they weren't nearly as polite to D.P. in their letters as they had been to Dougie on the phone. They told D.P. that Dougie Burns had a regional reputation at best, and a bad one at that. The only people in the population centres who knew who he was were the die-hard hockey buffs and they had better people to read about. For that matter, who was D.P. himself? He had neglected to furnish any publishing credits. No one at any of the publishing firms had heard of him.

Out of this series of blunt rejections, one vaguely hopeful comment stood out. One of the publishers had suggested that it would have paid more attention to the project if it had been submitted by an agent. D.P. took Dougie aside and convinced him that this was the way to go. The literary agency of Burns&Burns came into being.

Burns&Burns got right on the job. They contacted several publishers on behalf of D.P. Burns. They supplied these publishers with a few of D.P.'s completed chapters. In their covering letter, Burns&Burns expressed a lot of excitement about the book. Despite Dougie Burns's lack of national notoriety, they believed the book would sell well as a document about hockey itself. It was also an opportunity to unveil an exciting new writing talent.

By the time the replies to these queries came back to Burns&Burns, D.P. Burns had completed a first draft of the book. But Burns&Burns had also failed to inspire publisher interest in the work. The only tangible accomplishment was that Dougie Burns and D.P. Burns got an insight into how publishers and agents communicate. There was a chumminess in the publishers' letters to the agent, a kind of off-stage banter based on the common knowledge that writers are ego-mad, lazy and generally talentless. No one blamed the agent for this; a person's got a right to try and make a living.

We've seen as much as we need to of D.P. Burns's biography of the hockey player... what's his name? Oh, yes, Burns as well. Burns on Burns simply doesn't turn our crank. Frankly, hockey Burns should get a life before he inflicts it on the world and writer Burns should take a remedial prose course. Despite having to send you back your turkey we are delighted to find that your city now has a literary agency. Better luck turning up some talent there. Keep us in mind if you find something hot.

As any fledgling writer knows, the above process did not take place overnight. It took months. By the time it reached this stage, the hockey season was over and my first taste of retirement had begun. Many of the most bizarre events of my life were taking place ... but never mind. This isn't a story about my life; it's a story about writing a story, a story about being a writer, and I'm going to stick to that.

Being a writer, I was discovering, was an absorbing experience. Every day, at least once a day, I would leave the danger, chaos and boredom of normal reality; I would step into my office. This office was not a thing enclosed by hard surfaces; it was more of a mind balloon, a place made private by obsession itself. Then again, maybe I'm wrong to say it had no walls because, when I was in there, *something* stood between me and everything else. Obsession, again. Flexible walls of obsession surrounded me and all that could come inside were the pen and paper I was using to get it all down.

As you can imagine, this made me a lonely and strange creature to be around. Smitty Smith, with whom I had roomed on the road for my entire hockey career, was the most affected. He'd sit on the hotel room bed with his comic books; he'd want to talk or show me pictures – to "share," as the saying goes. But Smitty couldn't get anywhere near me when I was in writing mode. Through the walls of my office of obsession, I could see him, and hear him whining for attention, but that was about it. It was like watching a cat scratch at the far side of a thermopane window.

I don't suppose it will make me any friends in the community of writers when I say that writing, for me, was like being crazy. What went on up in my office (while I sat on airplanes, in restaurants, in hotel rooms) had nothing to do with what was going on outside. When I was in there it must have seemed to others that I had physically left, though my body was still hanging around. Once in awhile I might say something. It would pop out accidentally, out of the world in my office. Through the thermopane window I could see the embarrassed looks of my teammates and I recognized those looks as the ones I and my family used to exchange whenever my psychotic auntie got leave from the mental institution to spend a weekend with us. We could be talking about anything and, right in the middle, she would say, "Plants eat sunshine," or something equally weird and unrelated.

That's all I have to say about my writing process except to note that I hired a secretary to slap my scribblings into a computer. I selected her out of a handful of candidates because she could read my writing. Being an unemployed English graduate, Margo's skills went beyond transcription; she threw in punctuation and grammatical corrections for free. I'm pretty sure she had the same low opinion of my work that the publishers did but she had the sense to keep quiet. She needed the job; I needed not to hear that I wasn't doing very well.

Anyway, there it was. By the end of my last season of hockey, Dougie Burns, D.P. Burns and Burns&Burns had each taken a turn and failed to find a publisher for Dougie Burns's hockey memoirs. All agreed it was time the team had a meeting, time we sat down and talked frankly about the prospects.

B&B: We have to face facts, folks. This turkey don't fly, not on anyone's farm. We lose credibility as an agency every time we send it out.

D.P.: That's crap and you know it. The book is fine. Either the publishers aren't really reading it or it's ahead of its time.

Dougie: What am I going to do for a living if no one publishes this book?

D.P.: Don't talk to a writer about precarious livings, buster.

B&B: We could get some action if Dougie's career was a little more colourful. But let's face it: he's never been suspended for drug or alcohol abuse; he's never been sexually involved with a movie star. He hasn't so much as assaulted anyone in a bar or been named in a paternity suit. What have we got to sell here?

Dougie: I used to have the best teeth in the whole NHL.

B&B: Every milkfed kid in North America's got perfect teeth, Doug. In hockey, it just proves you're a wimp. The question is, what have you got to sell?

D.P.: I pen a beautiful book, an earnest, insightful biography and....

Dougie: If nobody will buy my memoirs, maybe we could do some other kind of book. I mean, we've got a team here, why not use it?

B&B: Not a bad idea.

D.P.: And what? Simply junk months of my valuable time? My blood, sweat and tears?

Dougie: How about a book for parents of kids who play hockey on the care of their children's teeth?

B&B: That baby's warm; that baby might live.

D.P.: A self-help book!

B&B: Yes, a self-help book, D.P. Think twice before you refuse. The streets are knee deep in out-of-work writers.

The wrangle didn't stop there. It went on and on. D.P. just couldn't get his mind around the demotion from biographer to writer of a tooth care manual. Dougie and Burns&Burns took turns soft-soaping him, Burns&Burns arguing that the book would sell and the royalties would buy him time to do his more artistic work, also that it would give him a publishing credit, however mundane, for other publishers to take note of.

Dougie made the more lasting impression, though. Taking D.P. aside, out of earshot of Burns&Burns, he assured D.P. that this needn't be your boring, point-form, self-help document. Dougie was not without some literary instincts of his own and he imagined a hockey tooth care manual with a twist, with a kind of postmodern spin on it. He also didn't see any reason why the tooth care information couldn't be spiced with dentally related titbits from Doug's life, which was to say, items lifted from the already completed memoirs. While D.P. didn't exactly cheer up at this, he seemed less inclined to quit in a huff.

The lesson everyone had learned from the memoirs, now a dogeared pile of manuscripts halfway up the extra bedroom wall, was that it was unwise to do so much writing before a publisher was found. Whereas the first project had proceeded in a Dougie–D.P.–Burns&Burns direction, the flow of the dental manual was to be reversed. Burns&Burns would now function like a football quarterback. Sometimes, quarterbacks run with the ball concealed; other times, they run without the ball, trying to look as if they have it. In this instance, Burns&Burns would run with the ball as if the agency had it concealed, when in reality the ball (the dental manual) didn't exist to be carried or concealed by anyone.

The process of finding a publisher was reversed in another way. With the memoirs, Burns&Burns had approached big national publishing firms, dreaming dreams of huge advances against royalties. With the dental manual, Burns&Burns thought in terms of a small, local publisher, one small and local enough to be impressed with Dougie's recently completed professional hockey career. Burns&Burns quickly found such a publisher in the Yellow Pages.

Fitzwilly Publishing Inc. RR # 2, Site 5. Books, Pamphlets, Wedding Invitations and Personalized Christmas and Other Seasonal Cards. Vanity publishing and family histories welcome.

Fitzwilly's last title had been *Old Fogey: Fifty Years an Oddfellow.*

D.P.: Not only do I get to write a dental care manual for hockey mothers but we publish with a vanity press.

B&B: Fitzwilly is the only publisher we could find who had ever heard of Dougie. He's a crazed hockey fan. He's had season tickets since day one and, by the look of his office, he can hardly afford it.

Doug: If he doesn't have money, how will we make money?

B&B: Truth is, Doug, we're probably going to have to put some of our own money into production of the book. But if it succeeds the way I think it will, it's money well spent.

Doug: You mean like money from my savings?

B&B: From your investment fund, Doug.

D.P.: So what about the writing?

B&B: Fitzwilly's in. Doug's in. It's time to get to work, D.P.

Over the next few days, D.P. produced the introduction for the book:

> *Hockey players have more dealings with their teeth than people in other walks of life. Whereas Doug Burns maintained a complete set of well-formed teeth through fourteen and a half seasons of amateur and professional hockey, his teammates tended to chip, break and spew forth theirs with almost wilful regularity. In a sense most hockey players have contempt for teeth, theirs and others, the way people will have contempt for video recorders if the ones they buy keep breaking. Having this contempt, hockey players are locked in an internal conflict. One part of them wants to rid the world of teeth, wants to knock out all the teeth they see and to spit out the last of their own. Another part is forced to acknowledge that teeth have uses, ones basic enough that if you lose them all you will have to replace at least some of them.*

Reading this, and seeing how pleased both Dougie and D.P. were with it, Burns&Burns made a decision: the agency would not bring Fitzwilly into things too soon, editorially speaking, at least. In discussions with Fitzwilly, Burns&Burns would concentrate on design and promotion. When Fitzwilly asked how the book was coming, Burns&Burns replied, "Marvellously." When Fitzwilly said, "Remember that our target audience is the concerned hockey Mom," Burns&Burns answered, "It's topmost in our mind."

The Art of Chewing

Of the uses put to teeth by hockey players the most complex is the chewing of food. You might say that this is not a complex matter and it is not for most people. But when it comes to chewing, hockey players are not like most people. When it comes to chewing, hockey players are locked in a mode of almost perpetual reprogramming. Doug Burns had come to know this by eating restaurant meals in the company of other hockey players. It was not uncommon, for instance, to witness food moving rapidly from front to back and cheek to cheek in search of teeth still able to chew it, not uncommon either to hear grunts of pain when a moment of forgetfulness caused the clamping of beefsteak between teeth recently ruined for that purpose. So many had run out of teeth, or nearly so, that players were often seen hauling out their dentures in order to pick at them with forks and toothpicks. One of Burns's teammates was locally famous for taking out his upper bridge in restaurants and giving it a hefty thwack against the table edge.

By now, D.P. Burns was again in transcendental writing mode, the state so like Doug's auntie's insanity. He never cooked, he seldom washed; when delivery people came to his door with pizzas, Chinese food, burgers and roasted chickens, they stood well back and took the other end of the money he offered so gingerly you could tell they were going to go somewhere quick and wash.

The only other visitor was Burns's old hockey ally Smitty Smith, and, when he found himself having to look through the mental thermopane, Smith's mouth formed the words, "Ah, shit, Dougie, not again." Smitty's job in hockey had been to protect Burns. Burns's retirement had left Smitty with nothing to do. He felt almost morally bound to retire and, besides, the team seemed uninclined to offer him a new contract. He had come to Burns for advice about this and about another weird thing that had come up recently in his life.

"Later, Smitty. I'll be done with this soon and we'll have a big talk."

"But, Dougie, there's this other thing. These two guys keep calling me. They want to...."

"Later, Smitty. Big talk."

"Ya, sure, Dougie, big talk."

Teeth: Their Other Functions

For a hockey player, chewing is not the extent of the need for teeth. Authorities will tell you that teeth play a role in speech and in giving faces their structure but, again for hockey players, the case differs. In the game of hockey, much more important uses of teeth are to display courage and to frighten opponents.

A recent NHL game supplies a useful example. A rookie who had managed to maintain an almost complete set of teeth through his pre-NHL career was, in the heat of play, forced to taste the blade of an opponent's stick. His hand went to his mouth. He stood hunched over. The trainer skittered across the ice bearing the rolled towel, trademark tool of the trainer. What passes for silence in hockey arenas was passing for silence in this one. Just as the trainer arrived, the boy straightened up; his hand came away from his mouth and in that hand was a sample of his blood and the broken bits of several of his teeth.

What then? What did he do? For surely this was a pivotal moment in his young career.

What the young man did was fling the bits of his teeth away and skate to the bench, glowering with great ferocity. In the next day's local newspaper, an important phrase appeared next to his name. That is: "Hormwood didn't miss a shift." The rookie had used his teeth to prove his courage.

After wholesale ruin has taken place in the mouth, a hockey player can go a step further. Consider this: you are leaned down low about to take a face-off against an opposing centreman. Your heads are very close. There comes that moment when you look up into the other's face. Right then, the one with the worst teeth will open his mouth wide. There it is: a mouth like a bombed city, its once-proud buildings shattered into ruins, broken pieces of furniture hanging out of exposed rooms, the whole works standing crookedly in a reddish rubble not instantly recognizable as a set of gums.

The person with this mouth is proclaiming something; a history of damage received and damage delivered; he is saying, "I don't give a hoot." And it's hard not to be shaken by that, for just that instant, the instant it takes to lose a draw. That is: your opponent has used his teeth to frighten you and gain a significant edge in play.

Fitzwilly was becoming suspicious. A particularly parsimonious man, the fact that he was putting up only twenty per cent of the cost of the book made him not one whit less concerned and nervous about his investment. "Marvellous" wouldn't cut it anymore as a statement of the book's progress; Fitzwilly wanted to see the manuscript.

On his next visit to the Burns, Burns, Burns&Burns literary establishment, Mr. Fitzwilly pored over the manuscript for a very long time. He seemed to be an exceptionally slow reader. The team of literary Burnses watched him read with a collective melon-in-throat sensation. When he got to the part that D.P. had written that very day, D.P. recited it in his head and still got finished before Fitzwilly.

Teeth as Determiners of Personal Identity

Up until the loss of his first tooth to hockey, Doug Burns had not so much as chipped a tooth. His interest in his teeth verged on the all-consuming: a deep-rooted, almost superstitious fear of their ever causing him pain combined with an unshakeable belief that he would never find a woman to love unless he kept the shelves of his gums completely stocked.

Chewing was something Burns did well, effortlessly, and he tended to show off that ease to his teammates as they ineffectually gummed their own food. Toward opposing players, though, Burns was careful not to show off. While playing, he would make do for oxygen with the air he could take in through his nose. In this way he concealed the good teeth which he knew would be nothing more than a provocation to the many goons in the league. This system worked well, up to the point where it failed to work and a tooth was lost.

Possibly there is a god of teeth, a god that hands out teeth and supervises their use. Chances are this god is no fan of hockey. Burns was attacked by a Montreal player, an unprovoked attack, a heartless act by a soulless man. When it was over, Doug Burns no longer had his left front tooth. Standing before a mirror, studying his impaired smile, Burns had both practical and metaphysical thoughts. Practically, he decided to plug the gap quickly. Metaphysically, he thought of the god he had offended. His brushing had lately been lackadaisical, his flossing sporadic. This was truly a vengeful god and Burns vowed not to offend it again.

The instant Fitzwilly put down the manuscript, D.P. and Doug Burns started up in nervous chatter. The substance of it was that the really good part of the book was only just beginning.

"You see, Mr. Fitzwilly, we're just now at the point where Doug Burns goes to the new dentist to have a new tooth fitted. It's really good there because he meets a girl. I mean, it's got romance, fear, suspense, surprise...."

Burns&Burns leapt in. "And lots and lot of good advice for hockey Moms about the care of their little hockey players' teeth."

But it was no good and everyone knew it. Fitzwilly looked old and sad. He had placed the end of his Bisons hockey scarf in his mouth and was sucking on it, loudly. He wouldn't look at anyone. When he finally removed the scarf, it was to say, "Doug, you know that, as a hockey player, I have a lot of respect for you."

It was a badly constructed sentence. Doug had learned to recognize them. Knowing he was doomed anyway, Doug said, "I didn't know you played hockey."

"I meant you. Respect for you as a hockey player."

A mammoth thought was rising in Dougie's mind right then, a thought about the word *but*. Wasn't it just the plain and painful truth that a person's whole life swung like some kind of noisy toy around the hub of that little word *but*?

"But I just don't think this book will appeal to the hockey Moms at all. It's so, so...."

Another portentous thought: that the next word out of Fitzwilly's mouth would slam Doug into a pigeonhole so tight he would never get out. Mixing metaphors freely now, Doug believed Fitzwilly's next word would be the one engraved on the headstone above his deceased literary career.

"Weird, Doug. It's very very weird."

In short, Fitzwilly withdrew his twenty per cent and, uncharacteristically for a vanity publisher, did nothing to persuade Doug and Co. to put up the total amount so the book could still publish. Fitzwilly was doing the Pontius Pilate with extra-strength soap and Doug was soon seeing the old trouper to the door, putting him back on his way to the house and printing press on Rural Route # 5.

With Fitzwilly gone, Doug became aware of a horrible smell and a terrible itch. He ran for the shower and kept it running until the bathroom was dense with steam. When he came out, he donned a bathrobe and a pair of rubber gloves. He made several high-speed trips to the garbage chute.

With Doug and his apartment smelling marginally better, it was time for the inevitable confrontation with his partners. Doug told Burns&Burns that he very much doubted he would need a literary agency in future. His future, if he had one, would likely be found in some hockey-related field, like car sales. Burns&Burns took it well, too well; Doug could tell that he'd dumped the agency about a minute before it would have dumped him.

Taking leave of D.P., his reliable old ghostwriter, was a harder thing. They had been through a lot, D.P. and Doug, soaring highs, crushing lows, and there had always been a great intensity of relationship between them. But for the good of both, it was time to part. Doug said that, as far as he was concerned, the manuscripts were D.P.'s; he should take them with him. Perhaps they really were before their time; perhaps they might yet find their publisher and enjoy a huge success.

That was the last Doug ever saw of D.P., the bedraggled scribe leaving down the hall, trailing paper clips and bits of manuscript behind him.

Doug was alone then, alone for the first time in months – but not for long. The intercom buzzer went, a berserk beelike whine lasting the full length of time until Doug got there to answer it. It had to be Smitty Smith for Smitty was the only person Doug knew in the habit of leaving his finger on intercom buzzers until he got results. Smitty was sweating by the time he barrelled into the apartment. He always took the stairs when the mission he was on was important.

"Doug, I got to talk to you. I can't wait anymore. It's real important."

"Of course, Smitty, no problem. I've got all the time in the world."

"You do? Well, like, I'm thinking I might have to retire, eh? There's nothing from the team about a new contract. So like I got to take any chance that comes my way, right?"

"Right, right on. *Has* something come your way, Smitty?"

"Well, maybe. There's two guys been calling me a lot. Sports reporter types. Man, this is embarrassing even to say."

"Go on, Smitty. I'm listening."

"Well, they want to write a book about me."

"That's good, Smitty. I think that's good."

"You think so? Jeez, I don't know. Like they want to call it *Smitty: Life of an Unknown Hockey Goon*. I mean, what sort of thing is that if there's a little Rodney coming along one of these days? A book like that about his dad."

"You've got to make hay while the sun shines, Smitty."

"You really think I should do it?"

"Given certain contractual considerations."

"Hey, what?"

"First of all, make sure they've got a publisher lined up and that the publisher is guaranteeing publication."

"I suppose, eh."

"If a publisher's in, you should be looking for a substantial advance. The writers will tell you they're the ones who need the advance but, without you, there is no book. Remember that."

"Wow, this is great, Dougie."

"Then there's the matter of royalty. I say you should get five per cent of retail, half the normal ten. It's not your fault there are two writers, you shouldn't suffer on that account. The same goes for volume escalators."

"Dougie, holy cow! Did I ever come to the right guy. How'd you get to know so much?"

"I've been many things in my time, Smitty."

"So what are you now?"

"That's an awfully good question, Smitty. That's probably the best question of all."

Colourful

CLARENCE MCCORD, VOICE OF THE BISONS, COMES TO
me holding his throat. We're in the commercial break
after the end of the second period.

"I can't do it, Dougie," he says.

"What can't you do, Cal?" Being McCord's colourman and
official sidekick, I have been instructed to call Clarence "Cal."
To do otherwise would be a quick ticket back to car sales.

"That Russian!"

A warm mist settles on my face. I imagine an army of
surprised viruses searching for cover in my pores.

"You mean interview him?"

Cal locks a hand onto my shoulder, squeezes the daylights
out of the little foam pad that the shoulders of our broadcast
jackets contain.

"Dougie, please. I've got to rest this throat. Else I could go
down in the third."

Cal has a head so bald and red you could believe that he was
the victim of a vicious gang-plucking this very day.

"Dougie, I'm counting on you."

Across the room in a zone of white light, the sweaty

Russian is sitting down on the interview stool. His tense guide and interpreter is avidly whispering at his ear, probably parsing the verb "to shoot" in an effort to prove that "shit" is not among its participles. While the cameraman fits Yuri with a lavolier, the producer is yelling a countdown.

"Nine-eight – would one of you jerks get in here – five-four...."

I race for the stool beside Yuri. The cameraman throws a lavolier at my chest. It falls into my crotch.

"Zero!"

When the camera light goes on, I have the little black microphone bud between thumb and forefinger. Raising it to my lips, I could be Gulliver, giving his first interview in Lilliput. Conscious of time passing in silence, I turn to Yuri.

Yuri is the first Russian hockey player ever to don a Bisons uniform. At thirty-three, he has played on six world championship Soviet teams. He and the Russian Hockey Federation are sharing equally in a good-sized NHL salary with no-trade and no-demotion clauses. In his first thirty-three games as a Bison, Yuri has amassed three goals and four assists. He is minus 19, meaning that the other team has scored 19 more times when he is on the ice, even-strength, than our team has. His eyes are set deep in his head and far too close to his nose: distinctly doglike.

"Yuri, what's your favourite restaurant?"

I don't know what's got into me but that's my first question. Maybe it's the fact that Yuri came to training camp twenty pounds overweight and has managed, incredibly, to keep half those extra lubs on through half a season.

Yuri is grinning. He is quick to grin, having never caught on to the fact that the media here is out to get him.

"Big Mike's!"

This is a surprise to me. Being penny-conscious in my early retirement (which is to say, poor) I know Big Mike's well, a not outstanding but very cheap takeout burger joint. It is owned by four Lebanese brothers who crowd worriedly behind their counter and wage a tense struggle to get the pickle and relish on your bun.

"You like hamburgers, then?"

"Cheese. Cheese bacon double-burger. Much like." Yuri pats a stomach that, alas, is visible even when slouching forward in a loose hockey sweater.

"What do you have to say to the people who call you an under-achiever, Yuri?"

Yuri loses his grin. He looks sideways into the shadows where his interpreter is glowering and perhaps wishing there was still a KGB to give my name to. Finally, he growls a word in Russian. Yuri looks back at me sadly.

"I try," he says. "Is no like play old country."

"But you always did well against NHL competition. You used to skate circles around me."

Yuri is a hard man to keep down. He is grinning again. I feel very bad for persecuting him like this.

"You? You play me?" He guffaws.

"I played four seasons in the NHL. With the Bisons. I played you in two exhibition games. I was assigned to cover you in the second one and you got a hat trick."

"Ya! Ya!" Yuri is very excited now. He is thumping me on the back with his big square hand. "I remember! You skate like old woman!"

With all this grinning, I am forced to look at Yuri's teeth. Meanwhile, to use the old hockey understatement for unbridled Canadian aggression, I am losing my composure.

"And you've got metal teeth!" A doglike look of Soviet noncomprehension. I rap my knuckles on my own teeth and point at his. They look like a set of used cafeteria cutlery poked at random into a ball of chewing gum. While I'm doing this, I happen to notice Mike the producer. He is alternately drawing the side of his hand across his throat and thumping the face of the stopwatch on his chest. I gather Yuri and I have overstayed our time slot.

"Well, keep eating those Big Mike's cheese and bacon double-burgers, Yuri. It will be a nice memory when you're playing for the Siberian Huskies. That's Yuri Gugilan, folks, Russia's answer to Orson Welles. Thanks for stopping by, Yuri. We'll be back with the Soundless Muffler House Out-of-Town Scoreboard right after this commercial break."

Cal and I are in the broadcast booth. Mike the producer is there with us, trying to give himself a heart attack.

"And if that wasn't bad enough, he mentions a restaurant – twice! – that has never advertised our games! Do you know how happy that makes the real, paying advertisers? There's a good chance this game could wind up being a freebie, Burns! Care to buy a spot? Maybe you could place a want ad for yourself!"

So like old times. Only then it was the coach who used to single me out for blame when a game had gone noisily down the toilet. I employ the trick I used then: the assumption of a kind of Zen state, achieved instantly without mantra by entire concentration on my carefully manicured fingernails and on quieter times in my life.

Usually these meditations take me back to happy little romances, ones that didn't scar me too badly when they ended. But my subconscious is less kind tonight. It has taken me back across town to Bonners's New and Used Cars, where, until a month ago, I sat in a small office cubby with mobile walls and a silk plant. Only the side wall of my office was a real wall and it was a wall of glass, a floor-to-ceiling window through which I could view the rows and rows of cars we were meant to sell. Mind you, I wasn't really meant to sell these cars; I was mainly there to reminisce about hockey with customers who remembered me as a player. Often these memories had to be goaded sharply by the salesman who was using me as a mid-negotiation distraction.

I am reawakened to the present by the strangled sounds of Cal trying to speak, to speak in my defence, at that.

"Mike, just F off, okay? So it was a disaster. Dougie had no brief. He was doing me a favour. You want to make trouble, you make it with me. Understood? With Cal. Get my meaning?"

The always welcome sound of Mike slamming the door behind himself. I turn to Cal and he is regarding me sadly. "That was awful, though, Dougie. I can't believe how awful it was."

"Fans like seeing Russians trashed, don't they, Cal?"

"Let's hope so, Dougie. But listen to me now. If anything,

this throat is worse. That means you got to do the play-by-play this period. Our roles reverse, see? Can you do that for me, Dougie?"

"I don't know, Cal. I've never done it before."

"Just say who's got the puck and where it's going. Don't try to keep up with the play. Wait and see what happens and then say what just happened. Get it?"

You may be wondering how I came to be chosen as a TV colourman. You may think to yourself that people absurdly knowledgeable about hockey are knee-deep on Canadian soil, and that the law of averages suggests that some of these must be fast-talking and articulate as well. You're right but also wrong to think that most of these folks are in the market for the job.

A colourman cannot be just anyone. He must be either an ex-player or an ex-coach. On the network, the colourman must be ex-bigtime: ex-NHL coaches whose teams won Stanley Cups or ex-players who won league trophies and scoring titles. Whoever it is must pretend objectivity about the outcome of the games.

Local broadcasts will settle for a lot less: usually, the best home team ex-player or ex-coach available. There is no objectivity rule. Quite the contrary. What is wanted is mindless bias. This limits the range of job candidates to those who have no hard feelings toward the old team. Because coaches so often depart suddenly in unfair, execution-style firings, local colourmen tend to be ex-players.

Now you have to find one who can talk.

Let's just say that while hockey players generally have some facility with one of the earth languages, most are not up to the stream of clean prattle required of a colourman. Hockey players spend most of their lives in all-male company, the company of men whose lives have also been shaped by the game of hockey. On the ice and in the team rooms, the words they are most rewarded for mastering are "Skate!" "Hit!" and "Fuck!" The art of goading opposition players into stupid penalties has a speech element too but here we are talking a language that, besides being unsuitable for television, is beyond the pale of civilization. This is soft underbelly talk, the isolation and ruthless exploitation of weakness, the product of malicious gossip probing back to birth and beyond. "Your grandfather ran away in the middle of the Battle of Ypres." That sort of thing.

Admittedly, some hockey players can talk but the sad truth about most of these is that they become bitchers. Unlike the majority who have the desire to complain, these fellows can put it in words. They bitch to the coach; they bitch to the press; they spend their careers bouncing around the league embroiled in controversy. When these kinds of players retire, nobody wants to know them, especially the people like TV broadcasters who used to interview them every chance they got.

So the bitchers aren't in contention for the job and neither, as a rule, are the guys like myself: the few who can talk but decide early on – and wisely, I think – that there is no percentage in it. Instead, we curse and grunt along with the rest while amusing ourselves with internal monologues not unlike this one.

The small remainder left by this process of subtraction are the team leaders. These are seldom as creative with the language as the bitchers, or as sneaky with it as I am, but they are terribly sincere. In the locker room between periods, they say the right things and they say them with passion and rage. Witness:

"We suck, man! We didn't hit shit out there! Now let's get out and kill somebody!!"

Then there's the sentimental appeal for greater effort in the name of a recently injured player or, better yet, a recently dead friend of the team.

"If Weeny coulda seen us tonight, he'da puked."

It is these team leaders, these locker room Castros, who form the usual nucleus of players from which TV colourmen for local broadcasts are drawn. All of which brings us back to the story because, at the beginning of the season of which I speak, Steve Burke (captain of the Bisons through all my playing years) was the local broadcast colourman for the CWAK Game of the Week.

It is my considered opinion that Steve Burke is a saint. Steve was born and raised on the Bible Belt but, not satisfied with being ceremoniously Christian from birth, he has been having himself saved and born again regularly ever since. As a player, he delivered crushing body checks within the rules but seldom fought. If someone fought him, he would certainly fight back but, if possible, he would wade in through the rain of blows and gather the guy up in a kind of friendly but firm Christian embrace. After his opponent ceased to struggle, the Stever would let him go, would drop him in a little pile on the ice, maybe even pumping the guy's chest a bit to get him breathing again.

On Steve's shoulders the mantle of captaincy hung like a sack of grape shot. He'd be the first one on the ice on game day, zooming backward around the rink. Being our steadiest defenceman he'd often play thirty-five to forty minutes a game but, if we lost, which we usually did, he would stay afterward to work at correcting some flaw that had cost us a goal against. Somehow, in addition, he managed to spend much time bent over the beds of chronically ill children. Training colourmen not to curse is usually the biggest obstacle but Steve didn't curse, wouldn't curse, couldn't curse.

So how did he lose his job? How did I get it?

What it was was terribly unfair. As a human being, Steve has no flaws; as a colourman, he had one. Steve is incredibly boring. It is possible that Steve could be entertaining, if he put his mind to it, but the truth is he has always put his mind to the opposite: to the dogged pursuit of being boring as possible. When you think about it, being colourful is often, maybe always, the same as being sinful. What do we mean when we say that someone has a colourful turn of phrase? We usually mean that this person is a malicious gossip who curses like mad. What do we mean when we say that someone has a colourful life? Probably that he brawls in bars, cheats on his wife and his girlfriends, isn't averse to a snort of the white stuff.

In his years of hockey, Steve Burke saw a lot of this colourfulness and he wouldn't have a bit of it for himself. He perfected a character so faultlessly dull that we couldn't help admiring him for it. In the storm-tossed confusion of our own lives,

Steve was always there in the distance – like Newfoundland. Immovable, unplantable, the seeds of change bouncing right off.

If you could stand the boredom, you could always pull your boat up on Steve Burke's rocky shore. His wife would serve you tea and cookies; his children would crawl up in your lap and pull happily at your face; Steve would sit in his Big-Boy reclining armchair and give you advice – "Gee whiz, Dougie" – long drones of sleep-inducing advice that sawed harmlessly on the surface of your head.

Steve must have needed the money bad to take a job called colourman but, having taken it, he wasn't about to stoop to being colourful no matter how much the fans complained and his bosses threatened.

"Jovilik carries to centre ice. He fires cross-ice for Eggwurt. Ooh, bad pass. In Eggwurt's skates and the Sabres take over."

"Gee, Cal, I don't know if I'd call that a bad pass. It's really hard to hit a fast skater like Bruce Eggwurt when he's at full speed. And you have to remember that Jovilik was about to take a hit from...."

"Play whistled down. It looks like Jovilik will go for slashing. Behind the play. Dumb Penalty. Still, it strikes me as a questionable call."

"Well, Cal, tempers do get up at times. I think Jovilik did strike Peckbone with his stick. Sometimes we can't see everything the referee sees. On the other hand, the ref can't be expected to see everything."

"You ever take a swing at a guy like that? In retaliation, Steve?"

"I'm sure I did, Cal, in a weak moment. It's hard to reconcile the teachings of Jesus with the moment-to-moment excitement of a hockey game. But in the penalty box I would always try to say a little prayer of repentance."

The fans wouldn't stand for it. The fickle jerks deluged the station with calls of complaint. So what if he was the ex-captain of their home team? Being endlessly colourful themselves, they weren't about to allow a man with a family to make a living if he couldn't be colourful too.

Steve Burke's reaction to being fired at midseason was typically saintly. He wanted to play a positive role in finding a suitable replacement. Knowing I was shilling in a car sales palace, Steve suggested me, which, of course, was a major blow to my chances of getting the job. Mike, I expect, tore at his nose a bit while Cal put his finger directly into the soft spot on this baby's head.

"Give me a break, Steve." Cal is fond of enumerating things on his fingers. "Number one: as a player, Burns wore out his welcome with the fans real good. Laziest bum I ever saw until they started letting Russians into the league. Number two: he can't talk. I interviewed him lots of times and he was dismal."

"Gee, Cal, I don't know about that. Dougie always had a nice touch around the net. Through those bad years, he was the team's highest scorer, although I'll admit he got very few assists."

"He can't talk."

"Sorry, Cal, but I can't agree with you there either. In private, Dougie has always been very well-spoken. And, you know, Dougie's what you might call … colourful."

Good old Steve. Colourful might equate with sin in his universe but he has always been most tolerant of the colourfulness of others.

I didn't immediately get a call from CWAK. Mike and Cal exhausted the alternatives first. Starting with a list of everyone who had ever worn a Bisons uniform or had stood behind the Bisons bench, they would have found that most of these people long ago left the city for warmer and trendier climes. Of the ones still around, they'd've found out that Beezer Ridner had nerve damage in his jaw which gave him considerable difficulty getting words like "shot" and "puck" out of his numb lips. Thermos Yupchik was having a little trouble with the bottle. He'd opened a bar called Big Babylon's and, every night when he closed the door after the last customer, he would sit in the immense, wonderful silence like a kid locked accidentally in a candy store wondering which bin to scoop from next. When they found Clyde Natlup it would be in an excavation somewhere, in the cab of his backhoe. If they were foolish enough to make him stop work to talk, he would ask about the money first thing and then would scoff, bragging of how he could make twice that much per hour right here in this cab and never have to put on a tie. He might offer to sock one of them if they didn't get lost and let him get back to doing real work.

I could go on but the point is they got down to the bottom of the barrel eventually and you know who they found when they did.

"Remember, Dougie, don't anticipate the play. Just try to be accurately a shade behind it. The viewers don't notice if you're slow but they get wild if you're wrong."

The players are down below, skating around before the start of the third period. I try to imagine describing what they're doing but I can't seem to find words for it. Then it's Mike counting down on our headsets.

"Well, Dougie, what about that second period?"

Cal gets the words out, lunges for his glass of water, swallows and massages the fluid down through his swollen channels. For the life of me, I can't remember the second period. Oh well, how different could it have been?

"I thought it was a pretty interesting period, overall. I thought I sensed the Bisons gaining momentum as the period went along. The shots were, let me see here ... ooh, the shots were Devils 17 and Bisons 5. But I really don't think that accurately reflects the play. I thought at times the Bisons were really into it, really coming on."

For some reason, Mike is yelling the name Flontineau in my ear. Flontineau. I run down the sheet of names. Yvon Flontineau, right wing, number 15, born Sherbrooke, 1968. I look around the ice for him. He doesn't seem to be there.

"Yvon Flontineau...." I say, sort of experimentally.

Cal raises his head up off his hands and whispers, "His leg."

"Oh, ya. Yvon Flontineau was carried off on a stretcher during the second period. We don't know the extent of the injury. He seemed to catch a skate...."

Mike's screaming through the wire into my ear, "He was checked into the boards from behind!"

"... while being checked into the boards from behind...."

"His f-ing leg is broken!"

"... breaking his leg in the process. We don't know the extent of the break. It would be a terrible blow to the team if this broken leg proves to be broken – well, you know, badly broken. You know what I mean. Not all leg breaks are the same. You have your multiple fracture, your clean break, your tibia, your femur, your hairline fracture, and alignment of the break is a big consideration...."

Cal lifts up again, brings his lips close to his microphone and says, "The game is underway."

And indeed it is.

Now, I've had various thoughts over the years about the art of play-by-play broadcasting. I've never quite understood why people need to be told what they're seeing. I mean, you don't take this approach when making a movie.

"He's picking up a dish. It's a blue dish. He appears to be about to either throw it at Ellen or dash it to the floor. Well, actually, he fakes at Ellen, fakes at the floor, and sets the dish back down."

Why is this more necessary during a hockey game?

My theory is that it's because hockey made its airwaves debut on radio. All across the land, it was a tradition to gather around the radio Saturday night and listen through the static as Foster Hewitt told you what you could not see. When the game switched to TV, some little absentmindedness occurred. It didn't strike anyone as silly to go on broadcasting the games, to go on creating verbal pictures, for people who were able to see it for themselves. And so it continued.

Until this minute, when I seem to have struck the old play-by-play edifice a revolutionary blow. In one master stroke, all this redundant banter is gone. I am not speaking and I will not speak until there is a good reason to. Cal is up again, not saying anything either, but his bloody eyes stare at me imploringly. Mike comes back on the line: "Burns, say something right now or die."

All right. Fine. Although I believe in what I'm doing, it is also not my way to force innovation on a world that is not ready. Let them have their accustomed diet of *see puck, say puck*.

What now? Cal is climbing his way hand-over-hand to the top of his mike. His lips form words, force them out upon the world. "He scores!"

"He did? Of course, he did! I was looking behind the play a bit there."

Mike's at it again in my ear, sounding for all the world like he could use a good exorcism. "The Devils scored! MacLean scored! From Stastny!"

"So the Devils score and that makes the score... let's have a look at the big board up there... Devils three, Bisons one. The Bisons better look out or this one could be out of reach. The scoring play, by the way, is Stastny from MacLean...."

"MacLean from Stastny."

"MacLean from Stastny. Of course. I thought Stastny got his own pass there but no, it was MacLean, all right. Picking the corner...between the goalie's legs. Your old five-hole shot. But it did sort of go in the corner because of the angle. But how about that Stastny, coming from Czechoslovakia so many years ago, skating across the Iron Curtain you could say, and how must he feel about his fellow countrymen and Soviet players coming over here freely now with not so much as a howdyado from the old KGB? You wonder if fellows like Stastny resent that. Or, on the other hand, are they simply glad that it's easier for the others than it was for themselves? It's really hard to know these things...."

There's Cal up at the microphone, valiantly if hoarsely whispering, "Play resumes."

"Yes, there's your old resumption of play. They've been up and down the ice a couple of times since the last whistle, the usual sort of thing, a shot, a save, a defenceman clears the puck out to centre, someone shoots it back in. Now they're struggling along the boards. That sight, it has always reminded me of a documentary film I once saw about jackals and hyenas. I mean, there's your dead carcass and who's going to come away with the juiciest bit? In hockey terms, you've got to have the player who comes away with the juiciest bit most of the time. As a player I personally preferred starvation but I have to admit the truth of the old adage that if you win the battles along the boards you usually win the game.

"Now what? We've got a stoppage in play. Must be icing or off-side or someone freezing the puck under his body. No, it's actually a penalty of some sort. Probably holding. You get a lot of holding in hockey. Slow players grabbing onto faster players. I used to hate that, especially when you're held in front of the net. People shooting the puck in there at close to a hundred miles per hour and some big oaf holds you.

"Now here's something I've always wanted to talk about to someone. I'm looking at the monitor here and I see that the cameraman has found a pretty woman and has her all framed up in a close-up. I've noticed that, when the cameraman does this, the play-by-play and colour commentators usually say something like, 'Hubba-hubba.' Something really witty like that. But let's think about this for a second. Some women are probably thrilled to be on TV while other women probably don't like it at all. Let's face it. She's on there so the boys down at the bar can have a good ogle in the middle of the game. I bet nobody asked her if she wanted that.

"What I'd really like to do is discuss this further. If anyone out there knows the lady currently on camera, they might ask her if she would care to join me for a capo down at the Beanhead. No, wait a minute – let's just check who's advertising this game – how about for a Labatts product at the bar next door to the Soundless Muffler House? If she'd care to do that, I'll be there until midnight. But it's not a big deal. Really."

And there's Mike again. By the sounds of him his head must be doing a three-sixty around a projection of green bile.

"Burns, just shut up!"

It is very hard to please some people.

The moment when something ends. They're almost always sad little moments these, but, as they accumulate, they become precious. The small hinges where life bent sharply.

The game is over finally and the moment I am talking about is the moment of the end of my brief career as a TV colourman. Thinking back on it, I will likely remember how a ray of TV light was bouncing off Cal's skull as he leaned his ear close to Mike's angrily working lips. I'll remember the sadness that spread across Cal's face as Mike gave him the word, the word he will have to give me in a bar sometime later tonight.

Black spot for Dougie.

It must be remembered too that, in this moment, I am also sad. No matter how doomed the venture, I nurtured the hope that I would be a good colourman, would bring something new to the old art; that, over several years, I would achieve financial security and a kind of fame. Instead, I stand as nearly naked as Adam before the rocky wastes of reality. Again.

Here comes Cal and, when he gets to me, he does something unexpected, something else to remember the moment by: he asks me to pick the game's three stars. By the time the game ended it was a blowout, the Bisons losing by five. I give the first star to Tuscany, the Bisons's goaltender. Except for a serious sieving out in the third, he kept the Bisons in it. Second star I give to Flontineau. Poor bugger broke his leg.

And the third star of tonight's game is Yuri Gugilin: Yuri who the coach saw fit to sit out for the entire third period. This of course is mainly guilt. Who was I to get so on my high horse, accusing Yuri of sins I committed repeatedly over my entire career, with none of his world championships to show for it?

On the ice, the announcement of my stars doesn't produce much of a show. Tuscany chooses to stay in the dressing room. Flontineau is off in a hospital somewhere. Only Yuri comes out for his skate of fame. Under a hailstorm of boos and beercups, Yuri does a little one-skate pirouette, hoisting his stick, grinning like an industrial accident.

The sight of him thrills me. Yuri, who will not see another season in this league, who can't speak the language of this continent and hasn't a skill to vend in the real world: here is a man who looks out across a future much rockier than mine – and grins like an idiot.

With a heart explodingly full, I turn to Cal and give the old guy's foam shoulder pad a squeeze.

"What would you say to a beer, Cal?"

"Hello, beer."

Nunatak

Throughout his playing days and after they were done, Doug Burns was haunted by a missing piece of the puzzle of himself. Why had the Bisons used a first round draft pick to acquire him when they could have got him easily in a later round? Nor was he the only one who wondered; it came up in the papers every time he contributed to a Bisons loss.

A thing like that is very hard on a player. It can effect everything about him, including the frequency and energy with which he wields the floss and brush. It is like you are a prince but, every time your back turns, the whole court whispers a rumour that you are the barn cleaner's son.

(from the manuscript *Hockey Tooth Care: The Life and Times of Doug Burns, the Iron Bison*)

Angus Topworth sat in a green leather armchair in a pool of light funnelled down on him by a water-stained and tassled shade. It was a poor light. There were black spots inside the bulb as if moths had crawled inside to die. It was a hard chair, as if the flesh of a tough old cow was still inside. Angus Topworth perceived these things and, looking around, saw several other wealthy gentlemen suffering to read in a similar way, on hard chairs and under poor lights of their own. A club is a funny thing, thought Topworth, but uncritically. He had, after all, made himself rich largely to belong to clubs such as this, the more exclusive the better.

A club is a funny thing and Topworth stared again at the papers in his lap, the evidence of his having successfully entered another. The papers were deeds and titles and contracts having to do with his recent purchase of an NHL hockey franchise, paper guarantees of his membership in the club of wealthy folk who own professional sports teams – the club out of all of his clubs that had wanted Angus Topworth least of all.

Moving from the hard chair across to a cramped antique desk, Angus pulled a piece of yellow club stationary from one of the pigeon holes. He spread it on the ink-stained blotter and, selecting an antique fountain pen from an antique caddy, he began to entertain himself.

May, 1983

Dear Chairman of the NHL Board of Governors:

As to your board's concerns over my inexperience, yes, indeed, the facts have me neatly pinned. Prior to obtaining the Bisons, I had owned no hockey teams whatsoever. I submit, however, that I am not devoid of experiences to set on the positive side of that balance. Which is to say, I am an expert on horticultural transplantation.

The art of transplanting has two sides to it. There is the plant itself and there is the atmosphere to which one aspires to move the plant. My hockey team, a plant of a kind, was originally seeded in an environment entirely alien to it. During infancy it endeavoured to grow in conditions of heat and humidity dreadfully unsuited to its genetic material.

As a result, what I have received from the State of Louisiana is anything but a healthy plant. It is a plant limp in its pot, almost devoid of the signs of life.

From the beginning, I knew that my only chance of reviving this plant lay in the bracing climate and nordic soil of my city. Had it been given the chance to live here as a seedling, it would have thrived wonderfully well. Of that there can be no doubt. But that has also long ceased to be the question. The important question now is: can this plant, so cruelly neglected, thrive anywhere? Can it exist anywhere? These were certainly my thoughts and questions as I recently freed the team's limp roots from the Louisiana gumbo and transported it to its new western Canadian home.

While it is mostly too early to tell, I believe there are already some encouraging signs. To the nongardener's eye, these would not be apparent. The nongardener looks for glistening leaves, perky new shafts of green, and, of course, buds and flowers. A plant without flower is a failed plant in his eyes. But, as an experienced gardener, I look only at the root. Is the root spreading in the new soil, is it taking even the most hapless grip? If this be so, then leaves and flowers will come, all part of nature's arithmetic.

Yours truly,
Angus Topworth
Past President of the
International League of Horticulturists

By midmorning, Angus Topworth had moved to his downtown office. If his boardroom table were to be likened to a hockey rink, Topworth's preferred place to sit was at centre ice, opposite the penalty box. He was sitting there now looking at the spot on the opposite side where, in his opinion, his newly hired general manager of hockey operations should be. Instead, Dealer Dan Rapelli had chosen to circle the table and to sit beside Angus, leaving just one empty seat between them.

Dealer Dan had long arms and legs, also a long neck, appendages that stretched and yearned and swung from his body as if fighting to free themselves from the corset of his tight and foppish Italian suit. At present, his legs were splayed as far as the hinge of his crotch would allow. His body was screwed and stretched to enable his left elbow to surmount his right knee. While working out in this strange manner, he was also talking nonstop: about his qualifications as a manager and his aspirations for the team. He had just finished making the prediction that the Bisons would be a winning team in their second season under his control.

Angus Topworth sat erect throughout, facing the spot where Dealer Dan should be. Topworth's short forearms were on the table, perpendicular to it with the palms down. To silence his newest employee, he merely flipped his hands over, waggling them slightly side to side like puppies performing a simultaneous trick. Dealer Dan was soon silent and staring at the hands, wondering what they meant.

Finally, Topworth spoke.

"Mr. Rapelli, I would first of all remind you that you have the job of Bisons general manager. It is no longer necessary to talk to me as if you were striving to get the job. Second, though you appear to have a natural urgency to produce a winning team here, you needn't be in such a rush on my account. In life and business, things take time. I am a man of great patience."

"Well, sure, Angus, of course. I just thought...."

Topworth rolled the puppies.

"As your employer, I set down only two conditions. First, I have no great desire to meddle in team operations. For example, you will never see me in the dressing room...."

"Wise move, Angus. That's a helluva wise condition."

"That's not a condition, Mr. Rapelli; it is the preamble to my first condition. Condition one is that, on rare occasion when I do choose to meddle, you must obey without equivocation or delay."

"Well now, wait a minute, Angus. Hold your horses. As a seasoned hockey man...."

"That sounds like an equivocation or a delay, Mr. Rapelli, of which I have just said I will tolerate none."

Biting back words, Dealer Dan reached for the tuft of silver hair above his tie knot. He gave it what must have been a painful yank. Then, he shifted an inch down and began dragging on the knot of his boldly striped tie.

"Condition two: if my wife should ever call you and make some suggestion, I want you to agree immediately. Then phone me and tell me what you have agreed to."

Dealer Dan was virtually swinging from his tie knot now, like an ape on a trapeze, thought Topworth.

"Is your wife, I mean, is she the sort who's likely to do that? Phone, like?"

"You and I need never discuss what sort my wife is. Having outlined these two conditions, I will now meddle for the first time. You are familiar with this, no doubt."

Topworth produced a magazine from his briefcase. He pushed it across the table, still behaving in all ways as if Dealer Dan were where he wished him to be. The magazine was folded over and the page facing up glowed pink neon where Topworth had been highlighting things. Dealer Dan lunged for it and dragged it to himself.

"Oh, this damn thing," he said. "Bunch of crap, Angus."

"Let us be very clear about what this 'piece of crap' is, Mr. Rapelli. What it is, first and foremost, is an article in a recent number of North America's most influential sports magazine. The article is entitled 'Drug Abuse on Ice.' It refers to our team as it existed in the state of Louisiana.

"Now a bit of necessary background. Do you think the NHL wanted a franchise in this city, Mr. Rapelli?"

"Well, hell, yes, Angus. Why else would there be one?"

"Why indeed, Mr. Rapelli, but the answer is not that they wanted one here. Years ago, during the last league expansion, I proposed a new team for this city and I was told my application was the first one rejected. I was told that my city was so uninteresting to people in the North American population centres that an NHL team here would set the league's quest for a major U.S. TV deal back by decades. No, no, Mr. Rapelli, their wanting a team here had nothing to do with it."

After splaying himself expansively in the early going, Dealer Dan was now approaching his abundance of limbs from the opposite direction: he was trying to tie himself into a knot.

"There are two reasons we have a franchise in this city, Mr.

Rapelli. One: no one in Louisiana wanted to watch hockey. Two: this article about the team's addiction to cocaine. You follow?"

Above his elaborate self-bondage, Dealer Dan managed a nod.

"As surely as this drug scandal was one of the two things enabling me to acquire the Bisons, it is now the only thing preventing the franchise move from being a complete public relations success. This is a morally conservative city, some would say righteous and hidebound. It is vitally necessary that we assure our public that cocaine abuse has been eradicated from the team."

Now thoroughly pretzel-ed, Dealer Dan seemed either unable or afraid to move.

"Therefore, Mr. Rapelli, you will ensure that no player mentioned in this article ever puts on a Bisons uniform."

Suddenly, one of Dealer Dan's shoulders snapped, a sound like a dry stick broken over the knee, or at least that was the metaphor that came to Topworth's mind. Third-degree separation was Dealer Dan's diagnosis and he imagined a session of repairs with the team doctor.

"But holy mackerel, Mr. Topworth, that includes the only decent players we have. And, heck, a lot of those rumours were never substantiated."

"But, mackerel, heck. Are those equivocations, Mr. Rapelli, or would you class them as delays?"

Silence.

"Very good. You come to me with a reputation for making trades. I think this morning's conversation suggests an opportunity to use your talents to the full. You may take the magazine with you."

Dealer Dan galloped from the room. He had the magazine in one hand and was holding his shoulder in its socket with the other. When he had gone, Angus Topworth displayed to the empty side of the table the subtle configuration of his lips that was his only form of smiling. Just then, his executive assistant poked his head in the door and quietly coughed.

"What is it, Ashplant?"

"Mrs. Topworth phoned, sir. To remind you of your luncheon

engagement. I took the liberty of calling the limousine. You should probably leave in six minutes time, sir."

The subtle smile vanished without trace. A sudden tight squint, Angus Topworth's only involuntary facial tic, replaced it.

Estelle slapped her leather gloves down on the table cloth. Topworth could not help it; he squinted again.

"I took the liberty of ordering you a sherry, my dear."

Estelle took hold of the little glass. With the air of a cowboy in a saloon at the parched completion of a cattle drive, she launched the contents through her lips.

"Take the liberty of ordering me another."

Estelle had evidently been observing her show jumping class. She had on her jodhpurs, her tight peach jacket and a multicoloured silk scarf that frothed at her neck. Were they in a field, she mounted and he on foot, Topworth felt certain she would ride him down.

"How are your riding students performing these days, Estelle?" Topworth sometimes had to quell the urge to call his wife Mrs. Topworth or Madam.

"I hate it when you pretend interest in my life, Angus. It is such an awkward and pathetically obvious response to your knowing you are in my dog house, on my very shit list."

"There is some difficulty?" Topworth looked up but was unable to see. His eyes were clamped shut.

"Two times this morning, Angus, *two times* I was confronted with it. By two people who have every reason to look upon me with enormous envy."

A waiter came bearing menus. He bent between them as if asking to be struck on the head.

"Oh, go away!" said Estelle. She maintained her cur-kicking tone as she continued speaking to Topworth. "Our name, Angus, which I by diligent, decade-long effort have made synonymous with show jumping, dressage and timely endowments to the fine arts, you by a stroke of your pen have casually connected to a sport in which Neanderthal Hans Brinkers club one another senseless with sticks. Why go this roundabout route, Angus? Why not buy an axe? Why not directly chop out my heart?"

Topworth was muttering, could not help himself, words bubbling on his lips like little silver balls. "... publicity bound to subside ... owners not that important really...."

"Do shut up, Angus."

It is widely believed that the rich become rich because they crave and savour competition, the bare knuckles fight of it all; that wealth issues primarily from aggression diverted from the battlefield into the marketplace. The theory may even be true for most but it in no way accounted for Angus Topworth's millions, for his being one of the three most wealthy and influential businessmen in his province.

Topworth's understanding of aggression was that it was what you got rich to avoid. As a very young clerk in an agricultural implements warehouse, he had first noted how, as you looked up through the company hierarchy, tension and aggression seemed to intensify. By the middle management level, they had become almost unbearably extreme. But the young Topworth also noted how the aggression and tension seemed to peak at this point. As one looked higher still, they seemed to subside.

Young Angus could not see the top of the management mountain from his lowly vantage but, by a process of extrapolation, he was able to picture it as a zone of utter calm. *Nunatak*, he said to himself, borrowing a term from his evening self-education in geology and the other physical sciences: a height of land left untouched by the grinding, scouring weight of a creeping glacier. It was clear to Angus that he both wanted and needed to live in such a place of peace.

Aggression had a second meaning for Topworth. It was a form of human imbalance, perhaps the trunk from which the others grew. If Topworth had a single unifying business principle it was this: avoid imbalance in yourself; exploit it in others. When an old bull of business brayed in his field ("Damn the economic analysis, I'm going to keep my foundry!" "The hell if I can afford it, I want the damn thing!") Angus would calmly manoeuvre until he was in place to catch the falling bits of financially viable debris. It was by such a process that he purchased for a song a mysterious assortment of the implement factory equipment after the company's old bull had stayed in the field too long and been gored by a younger and stronger American bull. Angus had identified a pump at the heart of the company's old sprayer that was, with minor modifications, the same pump required in great number for the gas processing plants that were about to spring up all over the surrounding prairie.

If Angus had a weakness to go with these strengths, it was his weakness for clubs: clubs and all clublike phenomena. Almost certainly it had to do with growing up poor and being looked down on for the first half of his life, but Angus Topworth loved to belong to things from which most other people were excluded. It began with groups like the horticultural society. Then came the business and professional clubs. The richer he got, the more exclusive were the clubs within his grasp, and he was powerless not to grasp them. Eventually, this process led to the very heights of society and, particularly, to the heart of the province's most snobbish and standoffish family. It led to Estelle.

The story is age old. A family festooned with the attributes of class (in this case, an old ranching family) becomes simply too refined for business and, in the end, can only curse the infidels hired and put in charge of the fortune who have somehow conspired to lose it. *Class sans cash*. Before this situation becomes embarrassingly apparent, it is necessary to make good matches for the children (in this case, one child, an aging and indomitable daughter). A solution that has worked well in the past is to find *cash sans class*.

In other words, there came Angus, already a few million to the good in pump manufacture and rapidly acquiring petroleum exploration leases, groping his way to their door with an armload of roses.

It had turned out very well too, in most respects. Estelle had added much tone to Angus's life and empire, had certainly decorated both with much costly *de rigueur* stuff. Angus was grateful to Estelle and nothing short of dutiful. The only problem, one Angus had been quite ignorant of at the outset, was how imbalanced the ancestrally wealthy can afford to be. Having avoided aggression all his life, except to profit by it, Angus found himself married to a human Krakatoa, a woman who thought nothing of exploding outright at staff in stores, of throwing drinks in the faces of other society *grande dames*, of sending in a battery of Angus's lawyers whenever verbal and physical assault upon the enemy had not given her sufficient satisfaction.

Into his very home, Angus Topworth had introduced the living embodiment of the disquiet he had carefully constructed his life to avoid.

After his meeting with Dealer Dan Rapelli and his lunch with Estelle, Angus Topworth spent as quiet a day as possible. By evening, he had shut himself into his library and was reading a book for boys called *Skipper and the Hat Trick*. In this book, the hero, young Skipper Dooby, passes up his chance to complete a hat trick in the championship game in order to give an easy goal to a teammate named Slats Slavoniuk. Slats, so nicknamed because of his protuberant ribs, is the butt of many unkind jokes. He is the son of immigrant parents who have travelled to the big game in a horse-drawn cart.

Topworth enjoyed the book very much but then had difficulty melding its contents with a video of the last game played by his team at its old franchise address. There was a lot of fighting, a great deal of poor sportsmanship, and a generally selfish attitude about passing off in promising situations. In other words, there was no one vaguely like Skipper Dooby on Topworth's team.

Toward the end of the video and too silently to enable him to switch the machine off in advance, Estelle sneaked into the room and watched a bit over his shoulder.

"Fuck you, peckerhead!" she shouted into Topworth's ear. He squinted so tightly he saw stars.

"Pardon me, dear?"

"That's exactly what that baboon from your team just said to the other baboon from the other team." Estelle had learned

114

lip reading in order to better serve as a volunteer at a school for deaf children. Angus hit the power switch on his remote before anyone on his team could mouth more.

"Angus, I require from you a divorce."

Topworth dropped his head in his hands. As it happens, this was nothing new. Estelle required a divorce about twice a month but Topworth knew better than to act as if it weren't a serious statement.

"Oh my dear, you know that would break my heart." Though said without a matching interior emotion, the statement was true. Angus never abandoned a club.

"What do you think you are doing to my heart, Angus? By dragging this hockey team to town as a dog would the scavenged corpse of a muskrat?"

"My dear Estelle, it was one of my impulses. I admit it. And I do apologize."

With this, Topworth took a chance. Words like impulse had a curious effect on Estelle. She was capable of picking up something priceless and saying, "I'll show you an impulse!" But tonight she seemed more curious than enraged. She wanted to hear what Angus could possibly offer as a mollification, what kind of gift or promise he believed would match her fury. He turned to her with a book in his hand. It was *Skipper and the Hat Trick*.

For the first time in her life, Estelle was sitting in the bleachers of a hockey rink. She was not intentionally disguised but, in her fur coat and fur hat, she could have been taken at a distance for a giant mink. It was the hockey arena that Topworth's Bisons would play in when the NHL regular season got underway in a couple of months and, by then, there would be a well-appointed executive box for them to lounge in – if Estelle could ever be convinced to lounge there at all.

For the time being, it was necessary to sit amongst the residents of the town, an indignity Estelle was accepting surprisingly well.

"See anything, dear?" Topworth asked.

"Not even close." But her tone, Topworth noted, was more one of disappointment than chagrin.

A game ended. The teams shook hands and left the ice. The Zamboni crawled through a gap in the boards and began to make its wet designs in preparation for the next encounter. Managing to hold the book open with her fur mitts, Estelle passed the time rereading the conclusive chapter of *Skipper and the Hat Trick*.

Topworth left to fetch his wife a cup of coffee and, once out of her sight, he allowed himself to smile. He was standing under a high banner in the concourse. It read: WELCOME TO THE ESTELLE TOPWORTH INVITATIONAL FRIENDLY GAMES.

When Topworth returned to his seat, Estelle did not notice him at all. Her long straight back was tilted far forward. She had removed one mitt in order to place the tip of her finger into the valley that divided the point of her chin. The nail of this finger, long and lacquered, reached up to touch the bottom line of her lower lip. Her eyes were slightly squinted.

Topworth had seen his wife in this pose before, when studying horses in search of a champion, when producing her chequebook at an art exhibition. She had found something she liked and he followed her eye line to the teenage boys flowing around the separate halves of the ice in two opposing circles.

What could she possibly see?

But when the game got underway, Topworth could see it too. In the general melee, the feverishness of youth playing for the big prize put up in Estelle's name for this tournament, there was one fellow who stood out from the rest. Peeking at his wife's tournament program, Angus looked for the number and, yes, she had circled the name. Doug Burns. Could this be he? The redeemer?

The skating style was fluid, speedy, and generally away from the heart of play. A tall, lithe chap, his response to the game's action reminded Topworth of what happens when you thrust a stick down into an aquarium. Very fleet the way this one could dart quicksilver away.

Once when the puck came to the boy in his isolated locus, his patch of empty ice, he launched it into the top corner of the net with a kind of accurate and desperate quickness. Later, this caused one of the larger types on the other team to try and board him. It was magic the way the fellow virtually disappeared from harm's way. Then Topworth noted another important feature: how a linemate of the quicksilver one, a hulking left-winger with a lumpy face, lost no time cornering the one who had just tried to injure his linemate. Firing down his gloves, the lumpy left-winger pummelled the other fellow until the referee and linesman pried him off. Topworth noted the fellow's number and circled his name in the program. Rodney Smith. Seeing this, Estelle frowned deeply at Topworth for the first time all day.

At home late that evening, after the tournament had ended, after the trophies had been given out, including the Estelle Topworth Prize for Gentlemanly Play, which went to Burns, the quicksilver one, of course, Estelle finally challenged Topworth for his having marked the name of the bony-faced fellow who had dropped his gloves and fought.

"Rome was not built in a day, my dear."

"I hate it when you resort to cliches, Angus. Explain yourself."

"I agree entirely with your choice of young Doug Burns. We will build our team around him. But what if he should be badly injured before his effect on the game is felt? Would it not be wiser to bring along his protector, this Rodney Smith fellow, as well?"

"Oh, all right, Angus. When you put it that way, all right."

They were in the boardroom again. Topworth and Dealer Dan: Topworth at his usual position at centre ice; Dealer Dan directly across in the penalty box, with his wrists propped on the mahogany.

Dealer Dan looked as if he had not been well. In amongst the scars left from his playing days, a network of creases had begun to form. The circles under his eyes had darkened to such a degree that one might have thought he had resumed his old hobby of barroom brawling. Topworth and Dealer Dan knew better; they knew that the damage was being done from within.

"I don't know how much more of this I can take, Mr. Topworth," Dealer Dan was saying.

"I hope you don't mean more employment, Mr. Rapelli."

"I don't know what I mean."

"Do try to elaborate."

"Do you know how stupid it's making me look?"

"What's that, Mr. Rapelli, your suit?"

"When everyone else in the league is hard at it in training camp, getting ready for the exhibition season, I send my guys to the golf course for weeks so we can host an out-of-season tournament for juniors."

"Scouting for the future, Mr. Rapelli."

"What future?"

"The usual one beginning in the instant beyond any current instant."

Dealer Dan's bejewelled fingers went up through his comb-grooved pompadour. The ripping out of hair caught in the rings was loud in the otherwise silent chamber.

"I'm getting fleeced," he said appropriately. "The word's out all over the league that I'm being forced to make trades. I offer quality hockey players and I get offered shit in return."

"Language, Mr. Rapelli."

"By the time we begin the season, I'll have nothing."

"In view of these developments, where do you anticipate we will finish in the standings?"

"Where else? Dead last."

"That is encouraging."

"What!?"

"That means, does it not, that we will draft first after the end of our first season."

From the base of the void in which he was living, Dealer Dan struggled up in response to this remark. For the first time in weeks, he flashed his wolfish grin.

"Mr. Topworth, you cagey old cougar."

"I beg your pardon."

"You're throwing the season to get Mongo Prine."

"And who would Mr. Prine be?"

"Don't give me that, you fox. The most celebrated junior since Mario, that's who, and you're going to make sure you get him. Now, that is sharp. I mean, expansion teams do it all the time but who would have thought of taking an established team like this one and ruining it...?"

Before his next statement, Topworth considered calling security. But, looking carefully at Dealer Dan, so gaunt in his once close-fitting suit, the ball of silver at his neck going distinctly white, he thought not.

"We will not use our first draft overall to acquire Mr. Prine."

There was a hollow thud. It was Dealer Dan's forehead hitting the table edge.

"Mr. Rapelli, try to remember that this is a business. It is not a war. We are not inviting Hitler into the Sudetenland. We are merely putting on a sports spectacle for paying customers."

For a brief moment of final rebellion, Dealer Dan released his hands to wave and design downward funnel shapes in the air.

"But it is a game and games are meant to be won. People pay to see their team win. We'll be lucky to win five games this season and, if we don't even try to get Mongo Prine, how's it going to get any better?"

Angus watched this spectacle from his nunatak, wind whipping up dust devils atop the creeping glacier.

"Are you finished, Mr. Rapelli? Good. I don't feel it necessary, as you know, to give you explanations for my decisions. But in this case I choose to give you something in the order of one. First of all, let me say that there are games within games. At times, these are invisible games which must be won before the visible game can even be played. Do you follow me?"

Dealer Dan was rubbing the red mark on his forehead. He was rubbing it aggressively, causing it to pain, perhaps hoping to wake from a nightmare.

"The invisible game behind the visible is the one I am trying to win at this moment, Mr. Rapelli. If I do win, NHL hockey will be played in this city. Otherwise, perhaps not. Would you not agree that this is a goal higher than the winning of hockey games?"

"Ouch!"

"Will people pay to see the Bisons lose? Of course they will.

119

The Bisons are this city's first major professional sports franchise. For the first few years you won't be able to keep people away with barbed wire and sticks."

"What is it you want from me, Mr. Topworth? It's next year's draft, isn't it?"

"Very perceptive. Do you remember condition two of your employment?"

"Your wife?"

"That's right. You will be receiving a phone call from Mrs. Topworth sometime in the next while. She will ask you to do something and how will you respond?"

"I agree to do what she says and then I call you and tell you what."

"In this case we can dispense with the phone call. I already know what she will ask."

"What? Tell me, please."

"She will tell you whom you are to draft with your first two selections next spring. Mr. Rapelli? Are you all right, Mr. Rapelli?"

The following eighteen months were busy ones for the Bisons franchise. The team played its first season, lost regularly to full houses, and easily finished last in the league.

Dealer Dan made several complex trades during the season. He dealt away his right to draft first overall the following spring. In return, he received several players and some future considerations. Included in the future considerations were two draft picks near the end of next year's first round.

Dealer Dan proceeded to stun the hockey world by using his first-round draft picks to acquire two unheralded players from the same line on the same junior team: a high-scoring but soft and unrespected centre named Doug Burns and his left-winger, a bruising oaf named Rodney "Smitty" Smith.

Taking Burns in the first round was viewed as unnecessary. Taking Smith so high was regarded as insane. No one expected Smith to be drafted at all. He was not listed by central scouting.

Both players soon agreed to terms with the Bisons and, again mysteriously as far as the press and the rest of the hockey world were concerned, both survived training camp to become starting players as the team went into its second season. Approaching the all-star break of season two, the Bisons were trailing the rest of the league by a substantial margin. They were in fact considerably worse than in year one and were on target to break the league record for least regular season points in history.

Some might have viewed this as a bad situation but Angus Topworth was not among them. He was very pleased with the Bisons, or more particularly with his wife's increasing involvement in team affairs.

Thanks to Estelle Topworth, four of the Bisons players, including Smitty Smith, were progressing satisfactorily in a literacy and remedial English class. The team now practised to classical music on the loudspeaker system. She had set up her own international scouting system and was composing a list for next year's draft: a Victoria defenceman with medical school aspirations; a young Czech national team player who played the piano, and so on.

Doug Burns was regularly invited to the Topworth home for dinner. In keeping with the rest of Burns's life and career, Smitty Smith came along. "Rodney," Mrs. Topworth would chide, "I know your nose has been broken many times, but that is not a satisfactory excuse for making so much noise while eating soup. Try holding your breath when the spoon nears your mouth." Dougie was supplied with books from the Topworth library and had acquired a taste for Flaubert.

Then came the sad day when Dealer Dan asked to be released from his contract as general manager of the team. A mere shadow of the man who had once strutted into Topworth's boardroom, calling him Angus and sitting in the wrong place, Dealer Dan crept in now and sat meekly on the far side of the table. He looked a bit like a portrait in the blue-grey emaciated style of Degas.

"So, Mr. Rapelli, you wish me to tear up your contract."

"I need out, Mr. Topworth. I'm begging you. This job's killing me. It's killed my reputation already."

"Now, now, Mr. Rapelli, let's not be melodramatic. I will of course grant your wish but...."

"There's a condition." Dealer Dan sighed this quietly.

"Yes, there is. Believe it or not, I have some concern about my reputation as well. Hence, I must fire you."

Dealer Dan was as shocked as it remained in his power to be. Lacking the energy to flap about, he droned, "I'm crazy. The world is crazy. I'm locked in a madhouse."

"Not any longer, Mr. Rapelli. As of this moment I'm exercising clause 67.C of your contract and you are fired. The front door of the madhouse stands open. You may pass through it this instant or whenever you like."

Topworth pushed a copy of the contract across to Dealer Dan. Clause 67.C was highlighted in neon pink.

"But why, Mr. Topworth? Would you just tell me why?"

"Why what?"

"Why any of this? Why fire me? Why ice a team of sissies?"

"I suspect you know why I must fire you. For the obvious reason that I must have you to blame for our poor finish, for the bad draft picks, for the team. If I permit you to resign, it could be construed that I'm to blame."

"But you are."

"Of course I am."

"Why, why, why?" Dealer Dan was singing the words. His next suit might very well be white and lacking arms. "It's your wife, isn't it?" He asked this in a distant calling-the-wood-sprites way, rocking and hugging himself. "You did it all for her."

"Is that so very strange?" said Topworth. "I wanted a hockey team, don't ask me why, probably because the league said I couldn't have one. A challenge, you see. But what profit to get my wish if I were to lose my domestic peace?"

"I'd kill her."

"Would you really? But you see, Mr. Rapelli, I love my wife very much."

"Why is *she* doing it? Why does it thrill her so much to destroy a hockey team?"

"She's not destroying it. In her view, she's improving it."

Dealer Dan's hands flew to his ears, pressed them until his

head must have been nearly crushed. Topworth rolled his chair around toward the phone on the credenza. He called security and asked if they wouldn't mind helping Mr. Rapelli to his car.

An evening like so many that winter. The candlelight pluming around the Topworth dinner table. The crystal and silver all aglimmer. Smitty trying not to snort as he polished off the dishes as quickly as they came from the kitchen. Estelle pausing in her book talk with Dougie Burns to offer Smitty the right spoon, the right fork.

Topworth himself was not in conversation with anyone and he took advantage of the situation to peek at the *Spectator*'s coverage of Dealer Dan's removal from Bisons management. It was written by the local curmudgeon Pop Gunn and his headline read DEMENTED DEALER DEPARTS. Topworth noted with satisfaction that he himself was mentioned only once in the article. "Something obviously had to be done," he was quoted as saying.

Estelle recalled his attention when she stood up from her seat. She had a sheaf of paper in her hands and looked about to read something.

"I want your honest opinion, Douglas. This may be my only chance to talk to the National Association of Hockey Mothers. It's got to stick." She cleared her throat and began. "After years of endowing the fine arts and supporting international horse shows and riding meets, I was suddenly brought up short by something my husband said to me two years ago. He had recently purchased an NHL hockey team and I was extremely upset with him at the time. That is, I was upset until he said, 'Estelle, why don't you admit it? More people in this country play and watch hockey than will ever write or read a good book, more than will ever play or listen to classical music. If Canada is to be truly civilized, mustn't you begin by civilizing its major preoccupation? Mustn't you begin with hockey?' At first I thought he was mad. But then I stumbled on a book for adolescents called *Skipper and the Hat Trick*. In this book, a young boy with strong intellectual gifts, a generous heart *and* an affection and talent for playing hockey, competes for a hockey championship. In this boy, the finer things *and* hockey talent exist side by side, the one not seeming to interfere with the other. Estelle, I said to myself, why not?"

Topworth listened for awhile and then he drifted off. He drifted off and finally up into that place of peace, that landscape pinnacle atop his world where no phone rang and no orders were given nor taken. What no one but Angus could possibly know was that, even here on the nunatak, true harmony was not a thing guaranteed. How often had he come here only to be disturbed, perhaps by Estelle's voice braying angrily across the valley from her own pinnacle. But checking the atmosphere tonight, Topworth recognized one of those rare times when everything in his life really was in balance with everything else, when he had everything he wanted and none of it threatened.

Estelle's interest in hockey would not last, of course. Though they probably did not know it, Burns and Smith were not long for the Topworth dinner table. Sooner or later, likely sooner, they would be replaced by human symbols of something else. Stutterers, terrorists, self-hypnotists – who could possibly know? Whatever it might be, Topworth didn't mind. It might even be possible at that future time to work at making his plant, his Bisons, bloom. No hurry, of course.

Angus stared down the long table, down the silver-glittering corridor of white, at his tall slim Estelle still yelling animatedly at the hockey mothers of the nation in the guise of young Doug Burns. He stared at her and let the sound of her zither-like voice saw the air to pieces on its way into his ears. His heart filled to bursting. For a man whose pleasure in life is the alchemization of chaos into order, what better wife in the world than Estelle? What more reliable source of chaos in all of creation than his darling Estelle?

Hitting the Monkey

SIXTEEN MINUTES AND SEVEN SECONDS ARE GONE IN the third period of this hockey game. We are behind 4-3. In tomorrow's newspaper, it will look like a close game but the small crowd on hand here in the Dairydome know better. For most of this period, play has been in our end, as if the game was a party and we were the hosts.

The other team's goalie is making an exhibition of himself, doing a sort of dramatic pantomime about how little work he's getting. He takes his water bottle down off the top of his net every minute or so, either sprays some in his mouth or all over his face with his mask tipped up. Sometimes, he does the Ken Dryden thing and leans on the knob of his goalie stick. Other times, he does what another goalie whose name I've forgotten used to do: he puts his arms out over the top of his net, crucifixion style, and rests in that position. It really makes you want to pound one past him but, on the rare occasions when the coach calls for our line, the fourth line, we promptly get as bottled up in our own end as everybody else.

I know what I used to do at times like this. I used to dream. In my head I would rove all over my life, trying to make sense of it. I can't deny the need for such life-roving, such sense-making, still. For instance, here I am seven NHL games into a comeback and I really have no clear idea why.

I may not know why I've come back to professional hockey, but I can trace the timing of the urge precisely. It came on an evening in late June this year. I was home alone in my apartment and the solstice light had begun to get on my nerves. I didn't want a day to go on that long so I closed both sets of blinds over it. In the false darkness, I turned on my only friend: the provincial educational channel on my TV set.

What I was trying to avoid besides the light was the feeling that I should move cities again. For the first few years of my retirement, I stayed put in the city where I'd played my hockey. But an enormous tide of longing and dissatisfaction was building in me. Finally, it swept me away. It swept me over provincial, national and state boundaries. It swept me up and down major river systems, across continental divides and over mountain ranges. I never moved in order to move again. I moved in search of a place to stick. But I never seemed to.

I was in northern California when it struck me that I wanted to be back in Canada, not only in Canada but back in this city, the home of the Bisons, where I had had my hockey career. I felt this very strongly but again had no real notion why it was so important. When I did get here to Bisontown, I found it uncomfortably full of memories and strangely empty of people I knew. Even my old friend and cornerman Smitty Smith had moved away – or back. Smitty had moved with the his wife and two children back to our old hometown of Beaver Creek.

So there I was in June, watching the educational TV channel and trying not to think about anything save what was coming out of the box. In the past year, the province had had an embarrassing racist incident: a colony of white supremacists had bought a farm near the western border and had been burning a lot of good crosses, wearing swastikas and brandishing guns. The affair had gained national attention and the subtext of things written and broadcast in the Eastern media was, isn't it just what you'd expect out there, out there on the red-neck prairie?

To counter this bad publicity, the provincial government had given its educational TV channel an anti-racism hotfoot. The channel had scoured the world for documentaries on nonwhite people and a lot of these were about rain forest tribesfolk threatened by lumber cartels. I wasn't sure how these were going to defeat the province's cross-burning Nazis, but they certainly had fuelled a hatred in me for the international lumber industry.

The show I was watching that particular night was set in the Amazon Basin. It focused on a father-son monkey-hunting expedition. The father was a barrel-chested man who was said to be near the end of a great career as a hunter. His son was just short of puberty, a thin and wiry boy. They took up their blow guns and hacked their way into the steaming jungle. I was liking the show so much I popped my VCR onto record.

All that really happened through the rest of the show was that the father set the son up for a shot and he missed. Then the father spotted another monkey, followed him through the trees for awhile and knocked him out of the high canopy right at their feet. They took the monkey home and the father presented it to his wife. She went off to get it ready for dinner – or at least that's what I imagine happened. The show was over by then.

Back in the Dairydome, the game is down to its final minute. The score hasn't changed. We have a rare face-off inside the other team's blue line and Clement, our coach, has called a time-out.

We all crowd around Clement and his notepad, a huge thing on which he is drawing a diagram so increasingly complex it could be the formula for nuclear fission. Clement has decided to pull the goalie and, if I'm reading this thing right, he has decided to use me, the old power play specialist, as his extra attacker. At least, in the maze of curves and arrows, I see the letter combination F-1(B). B stands for Burns.

Surveying the circle of faces and finding mine the blankest, Clement asks, "Burns, who are you?"

"F-1(B), Coach."

"Correct. What are your coordinates if we get the draw?"

"Red-3?"

"Wrong. F-1(M)?"

F-1(M) is a thirty-year-old Russian rookie named Muktov, one of several foreign players on our thoroughly modern team. Muktov lunges forward and studies the page. "Red-6," he says.

"Correct. And if we don't get the draw?"

"Red-3."

"Correct again. Burns, sit this one out."

In order to participate in the time-out scrum, I had climbed over the boards. Now I climb back, slide to the end and sit. I have been retired from hockey for five years but I often feel like hockey's version of Rip Van Winkle. I can remember when there were no time-outs in hockey. I can remember when coaches called you by your last name or your nickname, or "Shithead" or "Lard-ass," as suited the occasion. I remember when pep talks consisted mainly of people screaming "Skate!" and "Fight!" and the short form for "Fornicate!"

I'm not saying those were the good old days; I'm just saying that, in so short a time, everything seems changed.

The monkey hunting show had a powerful effect on me. I was hugely moved by it. Tears were actually running down my face at the end, a bothersome situation if you don't know why.

All I knew was what I must do next. I jumped up and ejected the tape. I dug in the pile of other tapes under the TV stand until I found the one I wanted: an old, too-often played highlight tape about the glory years of the Montreal Canadiens, my only hockey tape. Except for some black-and-white stuff about Boom Boom Geoffrion, Jacques Plante and the Richards, it mostly celebrated the great team the Canadiens built around Guy Lafleur during the 1970s. I fast-forwarded through the oldest stuff until I was watching Lafleur, watching him do some of the incredible things it seemed at the time only he would ever be able to do.

It had just started being rumoured around the league that, after his first career with the Canadiens, and his first comeback with the New York Rangers and Quebec Nordiques, Lafleur might try a second comeback. He had been playing on a touring NHL Seniors team and it was ridiculous. He could skate circles around all of them. People never stopped telling him that he could still play in the NHL if he wanted. Rumour had it he would be back in the fall with the Nordiques for one more final season. One of the only hockey-related dreams I had ever had was to play just one game with or against Guy Lafleur. My rookie season was the season in which he first retired. He left after five weeks and Montreal hadn't played the Bisons yet. The first season of my retirement was the year he came back with the Rangers. I had missed him again. Maybe, just maybe.... .

I'm just stating a bunch of facts here; I'm not yet aspiring to explain my own comeback. The facts are:

1) I watched a show about monkey hunting and wept;

2) I watched the Guy Lafleur parts of the Canadiens highlight tape and felt aftershocks of the same emotion;

3) when finally I shut the TV off, I went directly to the phone and tracked down my old agent Bernie; Bernie who had recently been released on parole after doing time in the slammer for his second cocaine offence.

Clement hasn't finished drawing when the referee whistles for the teams to come back and face off. The referee drops the puck and our centre pulls it across, right onto Muktov's stick. Muktov moves it forward into Red-5.

I won't bother you with the rest of the code names and coordinates but I'll tell you that the whole thing up to this point is going like clockwork. Muktov's pass into the slot hits the pinching defenceman right on the tape of his stick. From there on it's not quite so pretty. D-2's slapshot misses the net by about a metre. It has tremendous velocity, though, and rebounds off the end boards all the way past everybody up the ice.

Possibly because of the unfinished state of Clement's

diagram, no one is covering D-2's place on defence. An opposing winger catches up to the puck and deposits it casually into our empty net. 5-3. Toast.

Clement's face appears over my shoulder, a little tightness and a blueish tinge to the lips.

"Coordinates, Burns, coordinates," he says.

"Right, Coach. Coordinates."

"Complete Interactive before you go home tonight."

"Right, Coach. Interactive."

When I finally got ahold of Bernie that night, my first discovery was that he was no longer in the agent business. That's what he told me over the phone from Toronto. He was selling software now for a young, government-subsidized high-tech company. "Strictly legitimate," Bernie stressed to me. "Entirely on the up and up. And I'm clean. Really."

There was so much paranoia coming through the telephone cable that I started getting a case of it myself.

"I beat the booze thing too," I told Bernie.

"You! You never drank."

"Not as a player, no. But I got the habit at a rest ranch after my nervous breakdown."

"Nervous breakdown! Holy cow!"

"But I'm sober now, you betcha. And quite sane, really."

We talked like this awhile longer, about how new and improved we both were. Then I sprang it on him.

"Bernie, I want to make a comeback and I want you to fix it for me."

The silence that followed was heavy. It was like a million ball bearings were rolling along that silence, like Alexander Graham Bell had just invented it and Bernie's next words would be the first words of a new age. Those were the sorts of things I was thinking, at least. A more probable vision would have been Bernie sitting in a little apartment in Toronto with something like an imaginary tablespoon piled high with white stuff hovering near his nose. I finally broke in with some very carefully chosen words.

"It doesn't have to be comeback for both of us, Bernie. You

wouldn't need to quit your day job, or any of your new good habits. All you have to do is give Mr. Topworth a call. Fix this one contract, line your pocket a little bit, and go on exactly as you are. What do you say?"

"Why don't you talk to Topworth yourself?"

"I haven't talked to him in years. I'd be afraid to."

"Why do you want to do it at all?"

"I don't know, I just do."

"Are you in shape?"

"No, but I'll start tomorrow."

"You been out a long time, Dougie."

"I know that."

"All right. I'll give it a shot. But keep your expectations really low. Absolutely as low as you can."

It is quiet and empty here in the Educational Centre, one of our team rooms far below ice level in the bowels of the new Dairydome. The Ed Centre is lined with personal computers and it is Clement's pride and joy.

I am sitting at one of the terminals about to begin Interactive, a program Clement created. Clement programmed it and it is programming me. Interactive contains 800 game situations which, by Clement's calculation, represent eighty percent of all situations in hockey. The players have nicknamed the software "Biff" and, right now, Biff wants to know who I am.

"F-1(B)," I type in. Biff is "player specific," meaning that when I type B for Burns, he presents a different speed and play selection than if I had typed F-1(M) for Muktov.

I push Enter and the game begins: a series of dots with letter-number combinations on them zooming around at near game speed all over the bloody screen. Suddenly it freezes and Biff asks, "Where to F-1(B)?"

Now, hackers out there may be saying, beauty, where do I get one. But consider this: if I can't make up my mind, I take a penalty which is added to my total time. I'm likewise penalized for pushing wrong coordinates. If, when I finish, my total time is over the "current acceptable threshold for F-1(B)," I have to start over. I could be here for hours.

And it's no good typing in "F-U, Biff." All that happens is Biff types back, "F-U-2, F-1(B). Start over."

Bisons owner Angus Topworth used to have a mysterious affection for me, ever since the Bisons drafted me about four rounds too soon leading up to my rookie season. This affection, unexplainable by mere human logic, and possibly erased by all the time and silence between us, was Bernie's and my only hope.

While Bernie talked to Topworth, and Topworth to his general manager, and Bernie to the general manager and coach, I stayed well clear. I worked out. I will spare you a description of the exercise program by which I brought myself back into playing shape. Suffice to say it involved weights, a running track, a year-round rink – and a great deal of throwing up.

Anyway it wasn't long until Bernie was back on the phone. His success was telegraphed immediately by his tone. The wheeling and dealing sound had returned.

"I got the call, Dougie boy. It's thumbs up."

"You got me a contract with the Bisons?"

"Hey, hey. Beam back down to the Enterprise, fella. Of course, I didn't get you a contract. Beelzebub couldn't have got you a contract. What I got you is a tryout."

"Oh."

"Don't you sound let down, you schmuck. Have you any idea how hard it was to get you that much?"

"You're right, Bernie. I'm sorry."

"It's in your hands now, Bucko. If you prove yourself at rookie camp...."

"Rookie camp! Not even regular training camp?"

"You heard me, rookie camp. Thing is, Doug, Bisons management wants proof you've got the guts for a comeback."

"Oh."

"You got to admit they got reason to doubt. So, that's me outa here, Doug. My only advice is keep your head up. Call me if you make the grade."

It's the day after my night with Biff. I had to start over four times and then I got too lucky: Biff assigned me a new acceptable threshold which I doubt I'll ever reach again.

Right now, we are in the midst of practice and I am skating hard through every exercise and drill. After about an hour of this, Clement comes off the bench. He slips and slides over to me. Clement can't skate. He has played about five minutes of hockey in his whole life.

"Burns, I've got to compliment you. I've never seen you work so hard."

"Do you want to know where I am, Coach?"

"Pardon me?"

"F-1(B) is in Blue-8."

Clement looks around in befuddlement, then grins. "That's right, Burns. That's absolutely right."

"If it's okay, I'd like to complete Interactive again after practice. I'm going for a higher threshold."

"Good, Burns, good." Clement's smile begins to lose something. "Do you mind my asking, Burns, why...why you're putting out so today?"

"Nordiques in two days, Coach. I have a personal thing about the Nordiques."

"I'm very happy to see you so inspired, Burns. And, if I may say so, seeing a veteran on the comeback trail working his, his tail off is a real inspiration for the kids."

"Thank you. I hope so. Could I ask you a favour, Coach?"

"Why, of course, Burns. Ask away."

"Could I play opposite Guy Lafleur Saturday night?"

The rumour about Lafleur's second comeback has proven to be true: the biggest news story of the current season thus far.

Clement plays a little Interactive in his head, bites his lip hard. "I had a different assignment in mind, actually, Doug." He sees my disappointment, goes through a life-changing experience of some sort. "Mind you, it would work, theoretically, now that I've moved you from centre to wing. Oh, what the hell, Burns. Hockey isn't all coordinates and science, is it?"

"With all due respect, Coach, no, it isn't."

"Yes, Burns, you can play opposite Lafleur. What's more, I

intend to tell the team and the press that you're going to. How's that?"

"That's good of you, Coach. Can I get back to work now?"

"Of course, Burns. Off you go."

Clement slips and slides away. He is so jaunty that he falls down.

Rookie camp was hell, a kind of designer hell modelled on my deepest fears: a potent and toxic distillation of everything about the male sex that will have to be bred out of the human race if life on this planet is to continue. Forty or so crazy-looking youths racing around on skates with the blades of their sticks held at neck level. They specialized in hitting people from behind in close proximity to the boards as if their best chance of progressing was to turn another young hopeful into a quadriplegic.

And Bernie was right: the old codger of slightly more than thirty on the comeback trail was the stone on which the young warriors lined up to grind their sabres smooth. I wore the longest plastic face shield money could buy; I found an elaborate mouth guard apparatus with a rubber toggle that I clutched in my teeth. I wore so much extra padding around my kidneys, I had to strip down in front of the coaches twice to convince them I hadn't arrived at camp overweight.

But such was the violence of rookie camp, mere armour wasn't enough. By about the second day, I had run out of cheeks to turn. It was time for counter-aggression, for the employment of dastardly techniques vicious enough to drive back this pack of snarling curs. I dipped deep into my veteran's bag of tricks and hauled out a chestnut called "playing with your head down."

You've probably heard this phrase before. In fact, you just heard it from Bernie: his advice to me to "keep my head up." Whenever hockey sportscasters want to explain why someone is suddenly lying senseless on the ice, they invariably say, "He had his head down." They imply that, if he were lying on the ice like that after having had his head up, it would be a serious matter; but, since he had his head down, it is entirely appropriate that he be lying unconscious.

My version of this is that I will at times *appear to be skating with my head down*. What this causes is an automatic response in all the violent and semiviolent players on the ice. Immediately, Pavlov's rabid dogs feel a stimulus in the reptilian cortex of their brains. Powerless to do otherwise, they skate for you as fast as their legs will carry them. Because I am only pretending to skate with my head down and am, in fact, peering around from under my lowered brow, I am ready when they come. At the last possible second, I leap from the path of the speeding train. If I am by the boards at the time, the in-coming freight will strike the boards with enormous force, sometimes breaking ribs, at very least driving every molecule of air from its lungs. One way or another I leave him lying on the ice, rolling helplessly forth and back.

In mid-ice, where the most video-worthy destructive hits are delivered to the head-down, the best I can hope for is that two of the freights will arrive simultaneously at the spot I have just vacated. Two of them lying on the ice, as thunderstruck and injured as they had hoped to render me. This is a true counting of coup and, when I had done it often enough, I earned for myself a measure of space.

But, of course, I didn't avoid all the hits. I absorbed my share. After each, I would force myself up and back into the play. What's more, I made damn sure the SS bastards who ran the camp saw me doing it. I also put the puck in the net often enough that they couldn't keep me from moving up, from going on to the real camp where the real jobs were on the line.

"Why do you want to play opposite Lafleur?"

It is the morning of game day. We are having a team breakfast after a light skate. Clement often insists on these team meals, at which we are all supposed to bond in new and meaningful ways. He usually brings an overhead, as well, so he can toss a few new squiggles on the wall. Today is different, though, and it is my fault. With a slight glisten in his eyes,

Clement is telling us for the first time why he has always loved hockey.

As a little boy, he couldn't play because of some problem with his feet. All the pairs of skates his hockey-loving father bought him tormented his feet with pain. So Clement worked as a stick boy, and watched and learned a great deal about the game.

When he lists off the hockey greats who were his heroes – Beliveau, Ratelle, Orr – all the statuesque and graceful players – he is starting to sound a tad gay. Not that I mind such a preference but, when he asks why I want to play opposite Lafleur tonight, the question somehow aspires to include me in his special passion, whatever that might be. With the whole team staring, I carefully reply, "Because he's a legend."

"Exactly!" cries Clement and something dribbles out of the corner of his eye. "He is a legend of the game that we love, and that's why we have to go out there tonight and beat the, the CRAP out of the Nordiques! Isn't that right, Burns?"

Clement has never said crap before, not to us and perhaps not ever. Though the logic of what he has said escapes me entirely, I feel compelled to agree. "Right, Coach. The crap, right out of them."

"Let's hear it for Dougie," Clement yells. "I know Dougie's going to play his heart out tonight. Let's hear it!"

A silence, and a long one. Livesay, one of our assistant captains, raises his hands and holds them palm-opposite. He fakes them together a couple of times while jerking his head at team captain Smollet. Smollet gets the message and starts clapping for real. The others join in. The fellow to my right at table reaches over and fetches me a hearty slap on the back of the head, driving my nose into my piping hot cup of coffee.

As the applause dies, I hear Muktov say to the fellow next to him, "I no get. Is Burns's birthday?"

To conclude the flashback portion of this story, Burns is now at the real Bisons training camp. The *Rocky* theme rises predictably to a montage of images: Burns fighting for his hockey life.

136

Possibly the underlying motive of all this is getting on your nerves: the question ringing in Burns's ears as he sprints thousands of lengths of the ice. Why? Why do this? Why all this agony? For what? It is possible you are saying: give us some credit, Dougie. We know you by now. Try money.

But, give me some credit too. I had looked at the question from that angle many times and, frankly, doubted it could be money. For one thing, by this stage in life, I had acquired a vendible skill. Back when my being an ex-pro hockey player still had some social and financial currency, I had been employed as a car-lot shill. While standing around waiting for the real salesman to introduce me as a distraction to potential car buyers, I osmotically absorbed a lot of know-how about how cars are sold. When my being an ex-pro faded from society's collective memory, I changed roles and became one of those actually selling the cars. This was my primary employment in the various cities I passed through after I had my nervous breakdown and my divorce.

In the game of good salesman/bad salesman, I was an effective good salesman. I was the guy who met you in the lot and took a sincere interest in your quest for the ideal automobile, the one who suggested you could get more for your old car than you had even dared to ask. After the bad salesman was introduced, the one who did the actual appraisal on your old car and found all the rust and hail dents, I was the guy who took you aside and fed you a cup of coffee. I was the one who called the bad salesman a real bastard and, rousing myself to believable anger, took him one last counter-offer. I was the guy who talked the asshole into throwing in the free tape deck.

Not a glamorous life, I suppose, but still a marketable skill in a world of cars forever changing hands.

Now look at what I had to expect from hockey. For all his zeal and tenacity, Bernie could hope to get me no more than a modest one-year deal. After he took his cut, it would be down to about double what I could make from a year of car sales. In less than a year, I would be back on the lot, living off commissions again.

When the final cuts were made, a week or so before the first game of the season, I was still on the Bisons roster and still didn't know why. Bernie hadn't kept his expectations as low as I had, evidently, because the lowliness of the contract he negotiated left him shocked and bitter. He seemed to blame me, as if I were the devil and he'd sold me his soul in return for a vegetable slicer.

Anyway, I got my old number back and, before our first game, the home opener, there was a little celebration at centre ice to welcome me back. A few of the older fans remembered me well enough to boo. I had a terrible game and was relegated to the press box for games two and three.

But whatever small measure of acceptance I have earned from my teammates during training camp and the first few games of the season is all going out the window tonight. The core of Clement's sentimentality has been exposed – by me. Meltdown seems imminent.

In the dressing room before the Nordiques game, he gives us yet another inspirational speech about his tormented feet and his mother. He confesses to a torrid lust for the Stanley Cup. He speaks with dewy eyes of retiring the number of a player named Moose Ochsenbach. Darting glances all round illustrate that none of us has heard of the guy. Clement explains that Moose was a gritty stay-at-home defenceman who played for the team at its old franchise address in Louisiana. Moose did not wear a helmet and a head-first slide to block a slapshot catapulted him into early retirement. Moose is still alive, Clement tells us, in a Manitoba nursing home. Ironically, he does wear a kind of helmet now, but on the inside of his head.

Clement carries on so long in this vein that we are late getting on the ice. The Nordiques are already out there skating circles, not just in their end but, owing to our absence, all over the ice surface. In dog terms, they are marking all over our home territory. To make matters worse, territorially, every single fan is chanting, "Guy! Guy! Guy!" But why not? This being the only Nordiques appearance on Dairydome ice this year, it is very likely the last chance any of them have to see The Flower play the game he used to own. I am rather proud of them for this.

Lafleur's line starts the game for the Nordiques so I line up opposite. I have never seen him this close up before except on TV. His hair is still long and he still doesn't wear a helmet. We're an odd combo, considering I wear every piece of protective hockey gear manufacturers make and money can by. Lafleur doesn't look at me at all, has all his attention focused on the ref's hand, the waiting sticks of the centres. When the puck drops, something like electric current leaps through him, ignites him into action. So begins an evening where much of what I see is the blades of his skates churning up little sprays of ice that hit me in the face.

Still in the first period, Lafleur gives me the slip at centre ice. He takes a long cross-ice pass at our blueline and unloads a slap shot that hits the post behind our goalie bang on. I've seen that shot a thousand times on TV and this one appeared to have much of the old zip on it.

"Lovely shot," I tell him next time we face off. Team captain Smollet hears this and gives me a snarling look. Lafleur's expression is more on the puzzled side.

With a minute left in the first, I'm going for a loose puck in their end and Lafleur skates me off. The play turns quickly up-ice and all the officials turn with it. This is what I've been waiting for. I put my forearm around Lafleur's chest and, gently as possible, mug him to the ice.

"Sorry about that, Guy, but I was just wondering if you remembered me at all."

"Get off me."

"Doug Burns? The guy a reporter said could go into the corners with eggs in his hockey pants and never break a one?"

"I remember the line. I don't remember you."

"Well, no matter. I was just wondering...."

"Get off!"

Remarkably, when the ref sees Lafleur wrestling to get away from me, he thinks we are fighting. He gives us both two minute minors for roughing. Skating near Lafleur toward the penalty box, I say, "Hope that doesn't scotch the Lady Byng for you."

"You're nuts," he says. "Stay away from me."

In between periods – we're behind 1-0 by the way – Clement

tries to makes something of the roughing incident, claiming my chippy play should be viewed as inspirational. Smollet grumps aloud, "I'd be more inspired if he scored a goal."

Smollet's insult turns out to be a prophecy of a kind. In the early minutes of the second period, I employ one of my more reliable hockey tricks. I have a kind of gift for appearing more ineffectual than I really am. I can, at times, convince an entire opposing team that I have no hockey skills at all. At the start of the second, the Nordiques have an edge in play and Lafleur is getting away from me regularly. Except for some really inept passing by his team, he should have a goal by now. But my old possum play is working on him as well. During an offensive rush, I swerve onto my wrong wing and, thereby, achieve several unchecked seconds off the corner of the Nordiques' crease. A rebound comes right to my stick and I stuff it under the diving goalie. 1-1. By the look on Lafleur's face, I'd say I'm really getting on his nerves.

Between the second and third periods, there's another bad moment with Clement. He wants us all to kneel down and pray. No one moves. Still feeling that I'm to blame, I say, "You probably didn't know this, Coach, but I'm a Muslim. I couldn't in all conscience say a Christian prayer."

Clement is persistent. "There must be some prayer we can all say."

Muktov to the rescue. "I no believe God. He dead."

Clement looks crushed.

"A little suggestion, Coach?"

"Yes, Burns?"

"What's a prayer after all but a common wish expressed?"

"Yes?"

"So couldn't we all just commonly wish to beat the crap out of the Nordiques?"

"I suppose...."

"Good. All together now...."

During the third period, I get the feeling, the feeling that this game which seemed very long when it started is now very short and soon to be finished. As the sportscasters never tire of saying: the clock has become my enemy. I try and try to get close to Guy Lafleur but he keeps skating away from me. My younger legs are tiring while his seem, if anything, to be getting stronger. I must do something now, I tell myself. I must instigate!

"Instigate" is probably the longest word you'll commonly find in a hockey player's vocabulary. What's more, we all know what it means: it means to start a fight.

Given that I have spent my whole career avoiding fights, starting them is hardly my specialty; and yet I know what to do. The surest way is to rough up a small player, a goalie, a good player, or a player who doesn't fight. In short, it means I must rough up Guy Lafleur.

The next time Lafleur and I are near a corner, I run him. I don't run him very hard; in fact, I make sure that most of the impact is me hitting the boards beside him. Then I give him a little shove on the shoulder. He gives me a little shove back and we're in business.

A giant enraged meathead whose job is to protect Lafleur steams over, flinging off his gloves. A dog-like tangle of spit and obscenity swarms from his mouth. Now comes the hard part: I must let him hit me. He winds one hand into my sweater, cocks the other fist back and moves it around. Similar to what you'd do on a penalty shot or a clear-cut breakaway, he has time and is deciding exactly where to let me have it. On my part, split-second timing is required. When the fist does come, I jerk my face down. There's a sundering impact of knuckles on plastic as he nails me on the top of the helmet.

After this blow is struck, a new page in hockey's book of etiquette turns. I am now the victim of a bigger, meaner opponent, which means that one of the meat-axes on my team should race in to defend me. But, look out, the Nordiques goon is winding up again: an uppercut to get around my helmet defence. What's going on here? No one's defending me. Before the second blow can land, I collapse, an unexpected manoeuvre that jerks my jersey free. Our goon, who has apparently decided to let me absorb a few before intervening, finally does arrive and the donnybrook is on.

Meanwhile, I am on the ice, on hands and knees, threading

my way toward daylight through a forest of equipment-thickened legs.

This is as planned.

When I'm finally out, Guy Lafleur is easily found. He is leaning against the boards with his chin resting on the knob of his stick, looking peacefully bored. I skate very slowly in his direction, making no eye contact, trying to look as if I intend to skate by toward our bench.

"Get lost," he tells me mildly when I get too close.

"Pardon me, Guy," I say and, with that, I whip off my gloves and grab his sweater.

"What is wrong with you?" he asks, dumping his gloves and grabbing my sweater.

"I have a question to ask you."

As I had hoped, everyone else on the ice is waltzing with his darling and there is no one free to come to Lafleur's aid. At last, some time.

"Why did you do it?"

"Do what?"

"Come back again?"

"It's none of your business."

"I realize that. But it's important to me all the same. I'm making a comeback too, you see, and I'm not really sure why. Is it the money? Is it vanity? Do I still think that hockey will attract me a wife better than I deserve? Or is it even remotely possible that I like hockey?"

Lafleur is looking almost interested. "You going to make it?"

"The goal tonight helps. My agent think if I get between fifteen and twenty and keep my minus down, I'll last the season. But, come on. Tell me. Why?"

A linesman jumps between us. "All right, you guys, break it up. Lafleur, get to your bench. You... ." He glances at the back of my sweater. "Burns, you're done for tonight. Go take a shower."

"Would you just relax? We're having an interesting talk here until you interrupted."

"One more word, asshole."

Just as the linesman is pushing me out the gate, Lafleur

comes up beside. He shrugs and smiles. "I missed it, that's all. I really like to play."

As I pass through behind our bench on the way to the dressing room, Clement slaps me on the rump. "Good boy, Dougie. Highly inspirational. Good boy!"

Guy Lafleur slices past a Boston defenceman, picks the puck off the boards, feathers a pass to Shutt in the high slot. He one times it. Goal. Lafleur goes end to end, pops the puck through a Detroit defenceman's feet, ducks round him, picks the puck up and fires it. Goal. Pete Mahovlich carries the puck straight down the middle, is sandwiched by the New York Rangers defence. Lafleur picks up the loose puck, fakes the goalie down and drops it back to Mahovlich with the whole right side of the net gaping.

The screen goes blizzard grey, then black. There is a flipping sound inside the VCR. I hit power on the remote. On the now blank screen, I continue to see things. Lafleur scoring and setting up pretty goals, the aging Amazonian hunter, blow pipe to his lips – and me, I see me too, stuffing that goal under the sprawling Nordiques goalie.

Then, for some reason, it's old Smitty Smith I'm seeing, my old cornerman. Smitty, who so seldom scored even in practice, is shooting from centre ice at an empty net. He nicks it off the post but it goes in, completing the only hat trick he ever got as a pro. I remember how, in his excitement, he lost control of his legs and fell to his knees, how he slid all the way past the goal into the end boards and had to crawl back on hands and knees to retrieve the puck from the net.

Smitty's wild look of happiness, the peaceful but satisfied look Lafleur would get after a pretty goal, the look of pride on the hunter's face when the monkey plummeted from the sky – what I must have looked like stuffing the puck under that goalie tonight. Is it possible? Could the reason I've returned to hockey really be that I enjoy hitting the monkey?

Sitting in the only armchair in my chilly apartment watching the empty TV screen, I see a lot of other things now: a NASA team doing high fives as the Space Shuttle lifts off; research scientists hugging each other when a diseased rat displays an increased immunity to infection.

Then I'm having a fantasy of myself as a motivational speaker, facing a sea of people that flows away so far it becomes an indistinguishable mass. Being as new age and sensitive as the next guy, I have amended my metaphor so it is no longer a hunting one. I am telling them, "I came back to hockey for the same reason it gives pleasure to sink a long birdy putt. Not everyone's birdy putt is as important as everyone else's, I realize, but you sink the putt that is yours to sink." Which is to say in less politically correct language: you hit the monkey that nature has given you to hit.

It is a rare and glorious moment, one in which I feel almost wise.

By the time I have brushed and flossed, and am lying in bed, I am already not so sure of any of this but that's okay too. To the previous pearl of motivational wisdom, I add: the secret of success is low goals.

What a marvellously poor choice of words for a hockey audience, I think, and it seems immensely funny to me. That's how it ends: with me in bed, alone, tasting the mint on my good teeth, and chuckling merrily away.

About the author

Calgary writer Fred Stenson grew up south of Pincher Creek, Alberta, where the chinook winds seldom allowed more than one month of river hockey per winter. His first novel, *Lonesome Hero* (Macmillan), was a finalist in Alberta Culture's Search for Alberta Novelist competition in 1973, and went on to win the Canadian Authors Association Silver Medal for Fiction. He has published a second novel, *Last One Home* (NeWest, 1990) and three books of non-fiction. Stenson's short stories have appeared in numerous magazines, including *Saturday Night*, *Grain* and *Chatelaine*, as well as anthologies such as *200% Cracked Wheat* (Coteau Books, 1992) and *The Rocket, the Flower, the Hammer and Me* (Polestar, 1988). His most recent collection of comic fiction is *Working without a Laugh Track* (Coteau Books, 1990).

About the artist

Rob MacDougall is a fast-rising star in the field of sports art. Since graduating from the Ontario College of Art in 1985, he has produced work for *The Hockey News*, *Golf Digest*, *Score Magazine*, *TV Guide*, *Beckett's Magazine* and Labatt's. He has been the weekly sports cartoonist and special events painter at the *Toronto Sun* for over seven years.

MacDougall's originals and limited edition prints are often used for fundraisers, and hang in the homes of professional sports' notables, including Wayne Gretzky, Doug Gilmour, Pat Lafontaine, Peter Zezel, and Don Meehan. His work can also be seen in Don Cherry's Restaurant in Toronto.